BYZANTINE

The Byzantine Generals Play Euchre

BYZANTINE GENERALS | PLAY SOME EUCHRE

BYZANTINE GENERALS | PLAY SOME EUCHRE

By: Gerald R. Gray

Publisher: Trailer Trash Records, 1st ed. Knoxville, TN.

ISBN: 979-8-9882666-2-4

BYZANTINE GENERALS | PLAY SOME EUCHRE

Other Books by Gerald R. Gray

For Policy Nerds:

> Interorganizational Trust: Implications for Public Utility Commissions and Investor-Owned Utilities. ProQuest, LLC. UMI: 3449687

For Cryptocurrency Nerds:

> Blockchain Technology for Managers. Springer. ISBN-13: 978-3030857158

For nerd nerds:

Byzantine Generals: Out to Solve Some Problems. Trailer Trash Records. ISBN: 979-8-9882666-0-0

Byzantine Generals: Pearlfish Paradise. Trailer Trash Records. ISBN: 979-8-9882666-4-8

Dedication

This book is dedicated to my grandfather, Jacob Gray, who always tried to make those around him better people. Somehow, he knew to order my loner hand, as my opponent, more times than I could count. His euchre savvy drove me to be the best player I could be and to wring every tip, trick, and card flip out of this game. Beating Grandpa Jake at euchre was no mean feat.

I also must mention my siblings and their families. Euchre is a family tradition. Oh, you want to marry into the family? Better learn some euchre. You better be prepared to spill some blood as well.

The family has also had some epic euchre battles during what we have termed, *the Greater Western States International Invitation Euchre Tournament* (GWSIIET). You see, each year my siblings and father would head to the Rocky Mountains for our annual backpacking trip; within which would occur our family round-robin tournament for euchre bragging rights for the year. If you want to win the GWSIIET, well, you better bring your "A" game. The insights from those victories and defeats have made their way into what you have in your hands now.

BYZANTINE GENERALS | PLAY SOME EUCHRE

I also want to especially thank my brother David. David had a super annoying habit of winning the annual family euchre tournament. Although I would sometimes win, my claim to fame is coming in... second, the most times. Thus, when it came time to get someone to review the wisdom (and jokes) contained herein, I turned to David.

Thank you, brother, for helping create the euchre guide that will no doubt be handed down through our families.

I can just see it now:

Future child: "Dad, where did this book come from?"

Future parent: "Well you see, some of our ancestors were *super* obsessive."

Foreword

Why Euchre?

Because it is the greatest card game ever. Duh. You can have your Spades, your Hearts, your Rummy, your Poker... this is the game of the Midwest. But we'll let you play it too.

Why this book? Because it is time to pass the old knowledge onto the young's of today. Plus, it's an excuse to make fun of commies while we're at it so... win-win.

BYZANTINE GENERALS | PLAY SOME EUCHRE

Table of Contents

Introduction 1
Conventions in this Book 3
Euchre – The Best Game Ever 6
    Dealing 7
    Understanding Your Cards 9
        Trump 9
        Bowers 10
    Scoring 15
    Game Play 18
        Reneging and Capital Punishment 33
        Table Talk and Bluffing 34
Euchre Variants That Are Stupid 36
    No Trump 37
    Ace - No Face 37
    Farmer's Hand 37
Terms You'll Hear 39
    "You can always count on your partner". ... 39
    Short-suited 40
    Buried 40

BYZANTINE GENERALS | PLAY SOME EUCHRE

    Fishing For Trump 40

    Kitty 40

    Leading back 41

    Overtrump 43

    Protected (Left or Ace) 43

    Sandbagging 43

    Sent a Boy (To do a man's job) 43

    Throwing Junk 45

    Throw Off 45

    Trump (or trumping) In 46

Stupid Things You'll Hear 51

Principles (Not Rules) 52

    Principle: Conservation of power 52

    Principle: Part of the joy of the game 53

    Principle: If your team didn't order trump .. 54

    Principle: If You Can Take a Trick – Do It .. 54

    Principle: Secure Your Point First 57

    Principle: If You Make Trump – Lead Trump 57

    The "Stuck" Exception 58

Strategy 59

BYZANTINE GENERALS | PLAY SOME EUCHRE

- Should I call Trump? 60
- Should I go Alone? 65
- Stopping a Loner Hand 68
- You're Stuck – Now What?......................73
- When Three Points Is a Trap! 79
- Securing That Last Trick 90
- Should I order the opponent's right bower?90
- Should I order my partner's bower?...........94
- When Should I Throw That Ace Away........95
- When Your Cards Turn to Crap Mid-Hand...97
- When Do You Trump Your Partner's Ace? ..97
- When Four Trump Isn't A Loner 98

Other Scenarios 99
- Crap Hand with Lead 100
- Stuck – do you go left or right? 101
- Do you throw away that Ace?..................101
- Holding Four of the Same Suit with Lead..102
- Ordering your opponent's loner 106

Final Thoughts..108

BYZANTINE GENERALS | PLAY SOME EUCHRE

Introduction

If you're reading this, you're probably here for one of a couple reasons: Your family is from the Midwest, euchre is a blood sport, and you're trying to avoid getting killed. Or you have heard about this game that Midwesterners take way too seriously and want to learn more. No doubt you are of above level attractiveness and intelligence – indeed, one of the finer people that you know.

Or you just want to learn a new card game. Well, we're here to help.

I was sitting on my porcelain thinking chair one day, playing with myself… in euchre. While ruminating in my porcelain ponderings it occurred to me – I could help people. I'm a giver, so this appealed to me. But what could I write about? How about one of the most popular games played in flyover country? Oh – and I could show them

BYZANTINE GENERALS | PLAY SOME EUCHRE

how to play better – you know, by using this thing called logic?

"But what about the leftists?" my brain asked. "Well, leftists like games too… I think. But they're weird ones from what I've seen on Twitter (sorry I dead-named your app, Elon), but still, games".

But will the logic they learn in this game be able to be applied to life?

You never know my little leftists, you never know.

There's going to be a lot of logic in the following pages that will escape some. You might save some time by going back to dying your hair, or growing your neck beard, or maybe getting one of those stupid nose piercings that makes you look like a bovine (for those with a lower reading level - you might know this as a "cow").

This book is probably more for the rest of you – you may be dumb and deplorable, but you're at least trainable. Maybe. We'll see. I'm not optimistic.

BYZANTINE GENERALS | PLAY SOME EUCHRE

Conventions in this Book

The following figure shows the players as they will be represented in this book. You have the good guys (the generals), which will represent the view of you and your partner.

Opposing them will be the commies.

The circle "D" will be used to represent who the dealer is in any given example.

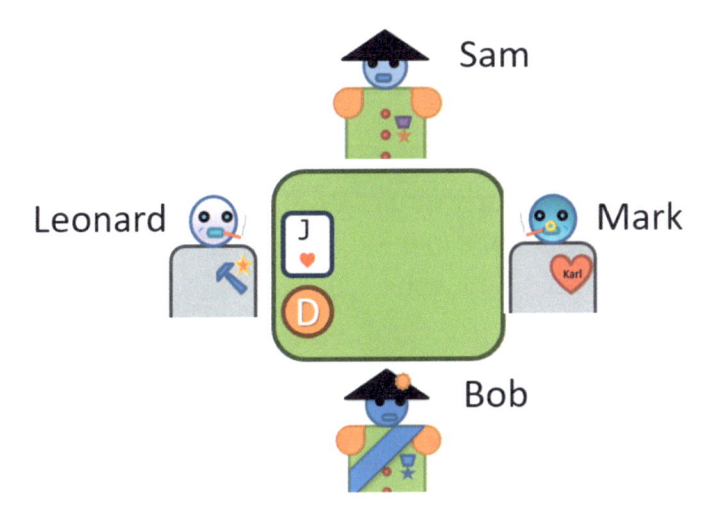

As an aside, these generals are not "generals", they are the computer metaphor "Byzantine Generals" from the comic of the same name. The

BYZANTINE GENERALS | PLAY SOME EUCHRE

comic strip that I coincidentally created. Hey, nothing says "branding" like overusing a concept.

> **THERE'S NO PLACE LIKE CAMP**
>
> "Metaphors hurt my brain."
>
> "Don't worry. There will be lots of pictures."

If you don't know what a Byzantine General is, go ask your weird cousin; you know, the computer science, cyber security nerd that doesn't have any real relationships.

Let's introduce our cast of characters, shall we?

BYZANTINE GENERALS | PLAY SOME EUCHRE

Bob – *The* Byzantine General – generally speaking (I'm sure you see what I did there). This general is the smartest, coolest person that you probably know.

Sam - Sidekick General – Loyal partner of Bob. Good partner that will never trump over your Ace. She's certainly better to have on your side than say, a communist.

BYZANTINE GENERALS | PLAY SOME EUCHRE

Leonard - likes long walks on the beach and wealth redistribution. Big fan of Bernie Sanders.

Mark – his favorite thing to do is central planning, that is, when he is not consigning his political enemies to the gulag.

Euchre – The Best Game Ever

Let's start with the basics. A Euchre deck only has 24 cards in it. You take a normal deck and remove the 2s through the 8s, leaving the 9 through Ace of each suit.

Dealing

Dealing is a bit different than other games. Starting with the person on your left, you can

BYZANTINE GENERALS | PLAY SOME EUCHRE

give them one, two, three, or four cards. But you must alternate, consistently, the number of cards given.

For example, as the dealer, if you give the first person two cards, you must give the next person three, then two, then yourself three. If you give the first person one, then the next person gets four, then one once again, then yourself four.

You do this until everyone has five cards. If the cards have been correctly dealt, there should be four cards left over. This is the "kitty." You then take the top card and flip it face up so that everyone can see it.

Always count the cards in the kitty. Always. If you turn that top card over, and someone does not have the correct number of cards, this will be called a "miss deal" and the deal is passed to the next person on your left (In the search for a competent dealer – or someone that can count).

You may be asking, "Do you cut the deck in euchre?"

Part of the joy of the game is the speed at which it is played.

Yes. If you're stupid.

BYZANTINE GENERALS | PLAY SOME EUCHRE

Why not cut, then?

Here is your first principle of the game: *Part of the joy of the game is the speed at which it's played.*

You can see this principle at work in so many aspects of the game; from how the cards are dealt in the first place, to how many cards are in the deck, to a "lay down" loner – or declaring, "I have the stopper" (see terms in the next section). Everything about the game is built for speed. One of the myths around the game was that it evolved in such a way because it was played on public transit in Chicago, and you needed to get through a game before getting to your stop. Another rumor is that the original deck included the eights and nines. What happened? My guess is that with the extra eight cards just took too long – and added too much variability. Smaller is faster.

BYZANTINE GENERALS | PLAY SOME EUCHRE

Deal the cards and move on with your life – and the lives of the other players as well.

Understanding Your Cards

This can be the confusing part for beginners. But let's walk through this step-by-step.

The normal strength of the cards goes from the Ace (being the highest), to the nine (being the lowest). That's the easy bit. Ace takes King, King takes Queen, and so on.

Trump

You can sort of think of trump cards as wild cards. Which suit is considered trump will change with every hand (we'll go over how this happens in a moment). When a suit is trump it means that any card of that suit is higher than any non-trump suit. For example, let's say hearts are trump. This means that a nine of hearts takes any non-heart, even an Ace of a non-trump suit.

But wait, it gets more confusing.

Bowers

If trump cards are wild cards, then the bowers are the wildest of the wild.

BYZANTINE GENERALS | PLAY SOME EUCHRE

What are the bowers? The Jacks - referred to as the right and the left bower. The right bower is the jack of whatever is trump. For example, if hearts are trump, the right bower is the Jack of hearts, and is the highest of all the cards, at least for this hand.

Ok, what is the left bower then?

The left bower (and second highest of all the cards), is the *jack of the same color*. If hearts are trump, then the left bower is the jack of diamonds.

Therefore, in the "hearts are trump" example, the trump cards are, highest to lowest:

J♥, J♦, A♥, K♥, Q♥, 10♥, 9♥.

Notice that with the addition of the left bower, there are seven trump cards in any given round.

Let's go through the other examples.

Table 1 Right and Left Bower for each Trump Suit

Trump Suit	Right Bower	Left Bower

Hearts	J♥	J♦
Diamonds	J♦	J♥
Spades	J♠	J♣
Clubs	J♣	J♠

Ok – we've got the relative strength of the cards figured out. We've got dealing the cards figured out. Now let's move on to determining what trump is.

BYZANTINE GENERALS | PLAY SOME EUCHRE

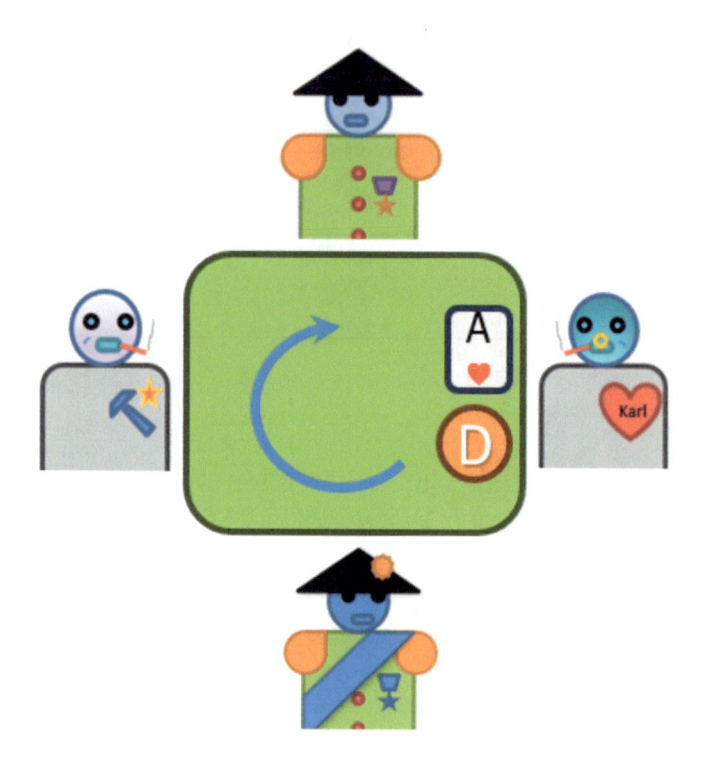

In figure 2, Mark is the dealer. The top card in the kitty has been flipped over to reveal the A♥. Play proceeds in a clockwise direction, with each person in turn deciding if they want hearts to be trump. If the player decides they want hearts to be trump they "order" it up by saying "that's trump," or something equivalent. If they don't want hearts to be trump, they simply say "pass," or they may knock on the table. Or they may say something such as "*I am disinclined to agree to such a situation in which hearts might be trump*". Real flowery types.

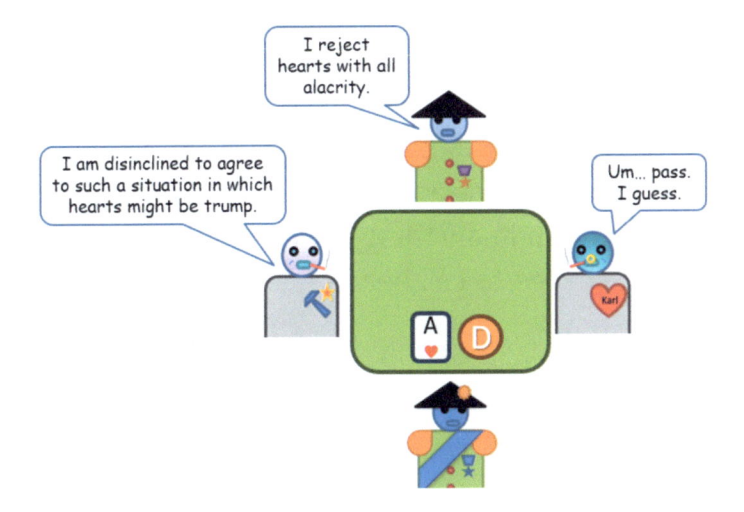

If a person orders the trump, the dealer picks it up and puts it in their hand, and then discards one of the cards in their hand and places it face-down on the kitty.

If play comes back to the dealer, they can in turn decide whether they want to pass or order the A♥ into their hand – this is called, "picking it up."

BYZANTINE GENERALS | PLAY SOME EUCHRE

What if everyone passes?

Then the dealer turns the A♥ face down on the kitty, and the next person in turn can decide to pass again, or they can call trump in anything but hearts. Everyone had their chance to call hearts – you don't get to go back now.

> So important that it bears repeating: *Part of the joy of the game is the speed at which it is played.*

What if everyone passes again? Then it is time to "stick the dealer."

Not everyone plays using the "stick the dealer" option. However, it is only children or other weak-minded fools who choose not to. Stick the dealer is reserved for those stout-hearted folks that don't fear what the cards may bring them and boldly call the best hand that their cards can support. Brave souls really. Also – *part of the joy of the game is the speed at which it is played*. We're not re-dealing the cards just because you're scared.

BYZANTINE GENERALS | PLAY SOME EUCHRE

If you're gathering up the cards and passing them to the next dealer (which is what happens if you *don't* play the "stick the dealer" option) for shuffling and a new deal... you're not really moving the game along, are you?

Stick the dealer – now let's play some cards.

Scoring

Before we get to determining if you should or should not call trump – let's determine what's at stake.

For each hand there are five cards. Thus, for each round there are five "tricks" that can be taken. To get a point, your team must take three of the five tricks (hands). To get two points your team must take all five tricks.

If your team calls trump and does not take three tricks, you have been "euchred," also referred to as going "set". When this happens, the *other* team gets two points.

BYZANTINE GENERALS | PLAY SOME EUCHRE

You can also go alone (without a partner). Which means that you not only order trump, but you declare "I'm going to go alone." Your partner (who probably wasn't going to be much help anyway) can now do something useful like collect the cards as you march to victory. Your team gets four points if you take all five tricks when going alone. If you only get three or four tricks, then just as with a normal hand, you only get one point.

If you get euchred when going alone, the other team gets two points, and your name and exploits get remembered for all eternity as an example of what not to do.

Table 2 Summary of Scoring Outcomes

Your Team	Tricks	Points
Called Trump	3 – 4	1
Called Trump	5	2
Went Alone	3 – 4	1
Went Alone	5	4
Euchred	1 – 2	Opposing team: 2

Nominally, you can also opt to defend alone. But this isn't practical unless you're playing in "purest mode" where a deck includes the Sevens and Eights (rumor has it this was an early variety in euchre).

BYZANTINE GENERALS | PLAY SOME EUCHRE

Game Play

The cards have been dealt with, you've assessed your hand for value and made your call. It's time to engage the orchestra and dance.

Trump has been determined so now it's time to play some cards.

The person to the left of the dealer leads. That is, they take

> You must follow the suit that has been led if you have a card of that suit.

a card from their hand and place it face up on the table for all to see. Each person in turn will then play a card in a similar manner. The goal, of course, is to see who will win that trick.

When the first card is played each person must follow suit if they have a card of that suit.

If a player does not have a card of that suit, they can either, 1) play a trump card, or 2) play a card of a different suit. Once all four cards have been played, the highest card takes that trick.

What is the highest card?

If everyone follows suit, the highest card of that suit wins. For example, if someone leads the 10♥ and everyone follows suit (meaning only hearts were played) whoever has the highest heart wins.

If someone didn't have a heart and played a trump card, then the person playing that trump card would win the trick, unless someone else plays a higher trump card.

If you can't follow suit and you don't have a trump card, you have what is known in polite circles as, "junk." Which means, you're probably not taking any points. However, if somehow you got the lead and played a low card like the 9♠, and if no one has a higher spade to play, or any trump to play, then that lowly nine will win the trick.

> The highest card that followed the suit that was led wins the trick, unless a trump card was played; then the highest trump card wins the trick.

The winning team collects the cards from the table and places them face down next to them – these cards are now out of play until the next hand.

BYZANTINE GENERALS | PLAY SOME EUCHRE

Let's look at a couple of examples. We'll start with a simple exchange and then look at an example where someone plays a trump card. Also, for these examples, we'll show all the players' cards so that you can see what card would normally be selected during the course of play.

In the following example, Bob is the dealer. Hearts are trump. In this example, Bob ordered the heart into his own hand. In other words, Bob "picked it up."

This means that Leonard has the lead (the person to the left of the dealer begins play) and gets to decide what card to play first.

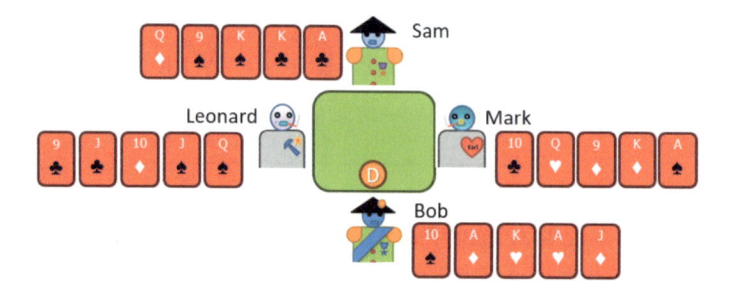

There's no way around it, Leonard has a lousy hand. No trump. No Aces. But he can serve an important function besides being a warning to other people. He can check to see if the person that made trump (Bob) is all red or holding some weak diamonds. Right, it's not much to go on, but it's something.

So, Leonard leads the 10♦. Play proceeds to Sam. Sam must follow suit, so Sam plays the Q♦. Mark must also follow suit but plays the K♦ to take control of the trick, rather than the 9♦. Bob plays the A♦ to take the trick (remember, the J♦ is the left bower in this case because hearts are trump, so it is considered a heart).

| Commies | 0 |
| Generals | 1 |

The remaining cards are shown in the figure below.

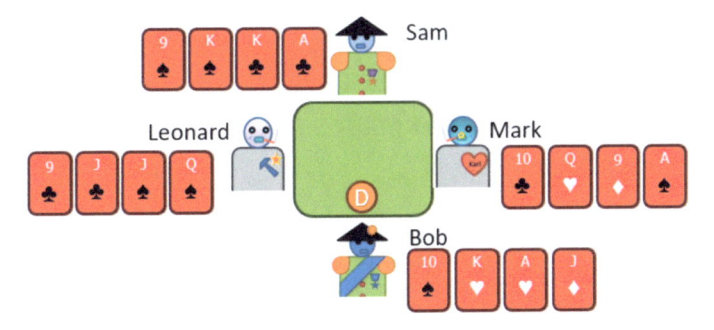

BYZANTINE GENERALS | PLAY SOME EUCHRE

Because he won the trick, Bob now has the lead. Following the principle, *if you make trump, lead trump*, Bob is going to lead his strongest trump, the left bower, which is the J♦.

Leonard doesn't have any hearts, so he can't follow suit. He can play anything he wants. He doesn't have any cards that can take the trick, so he gets rid of his weakest card, the 9♣.

Sam also does not have any hearts, so plays the weakest card, the 9♠. Mark does have a heart, so he must follow suit and play the Q♥. No one had a card higher than the left bower, so Bob takes the trick.

Commies	0
Generals	2

The remaining cards now look like the figure below.

BYZANTINE GENERALS | PLAY SOME EUCHRE

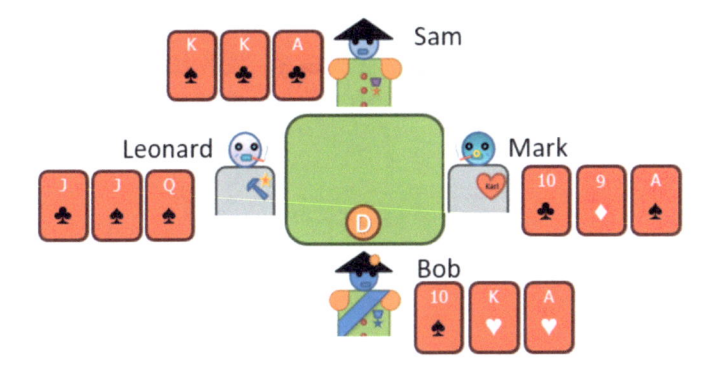

Since that went so well and the previous hand revealed to Bob that neither Leonard nor Sam had trump, Bob is going to play both the A♥ and K♥ in succession (knowing that if Mark had been holding the right bower, it would have been played on the previous trick).

Leonard, Sam, and Mark will play their weakest cards. For Leonard this will be the two Jacks. For Sam, the two Kings, and for Mark, the 9 and the 10.

| Commies | 0 |
| Generals | 4 |

23 | Page

BYZANTINE GENERALS | PLAY SOME EUCHRE

It looks bad for the commies. Bob might even be hoping that the Generals can take all five tricks and get two points instead of one. But it is not to be.

The setup for the final trick is shown in the figure below.

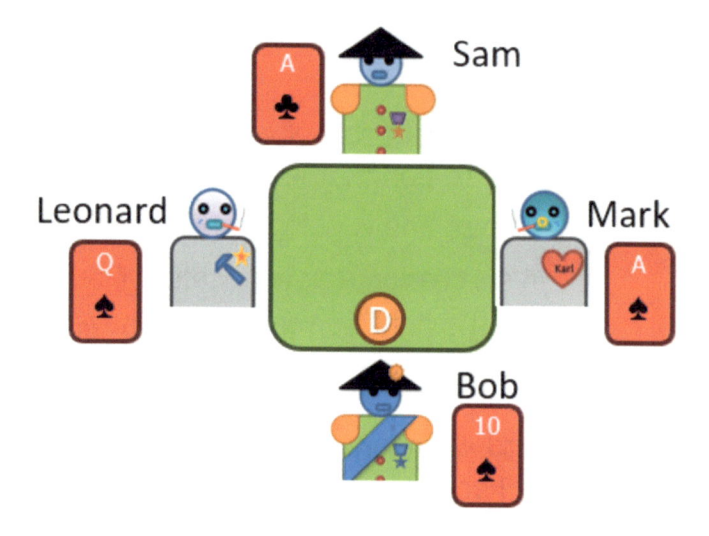

Bob leads his final card, the 10♠. Leonard's spade (the Queen) is higher. Sam's Ace is of no help, because although it is an Ace, it is not the correct suit and is therefore worthless because that wasn't the suit that was led. Mark plays the A♠, taking the trick for the commies (the stopper) and saves the day by preventing the two-point hand.

BYZANTINE GENERALS | PLAY SOME EUCHRE

The final tally of tricks is shown below – giving the Generals one point.

| Commies | 1 |
| Generals | 4 |

Let's do one more example. In an actual game the deal would pass to Leonard. This time we'll also consider the "up" card and decide who might call trump and what that trump suit might be. Remember, all the cards are being shown for the purposes of this example. Normally, the only card that would be visible at the start is the up card, which is the A♣.

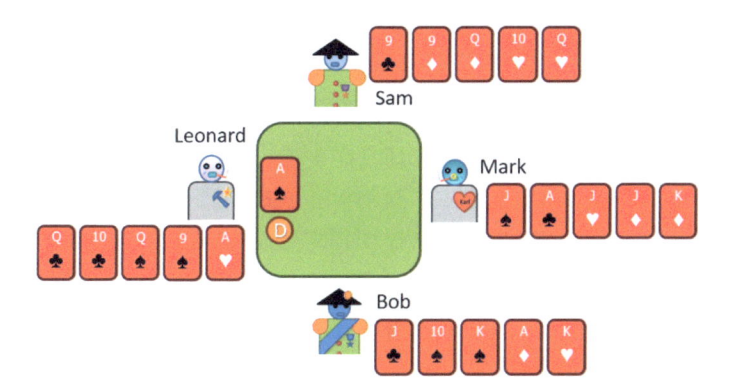

Leonard is the dealer, so Sam gets to decide first as to whether to order spades. Sam is looking at a weak hand and has no spades, and so decides to pass. Mark has what would be the right bower if spades were trump and has what would be an off-suit Ace, but that isn't quite strong enough to order the A♠, even though that Ace would go into his partner's hand. Remember, in a real hand he would not be able to see that his partner would end up with three spades.

Play comes now to Bob. Bob has a decent hand. If spades are trump, he would have the left bower and two additional trump cards (10, K), plus an off-suit Ace with the A♦. Thus, Bob decides to order the up card.

When a player orders up trump, the "up" card always goes into the dealer's hand. So, Bob doesn't get the up card because Leonard is the dealer. Leonard picks up the A♠ per Bob's call and then discards one of his cards, face down, on the kitty. Leonard will want to keep that off-suit Ace and his two other trump cards (9, Q) and so decides to discard the 10♣. The state of each hand is shown in the figure below.

BYZANTINE GENERALS | PLAY SOME EUCHRE

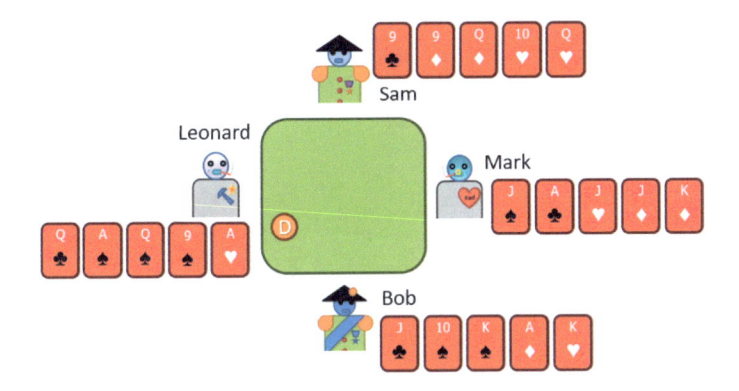

Since Leonard dealt, Sam gets to play first as the first person left of the dealer. Sam decides to play one of her weakest cards, the 9♣. Mark follows suit with the A♣. Bob doesn't have clubs, so he decides to play a trump card, the 10♠. He uses the lower trump card because he wants to save his stronger trump cards for later. Because clubs were led by Sam, Leonard must follow suit and play the Q♣. The play is shown in the figure below.

BYZANTINE GENERALS | PLAY SOME EUCHRE

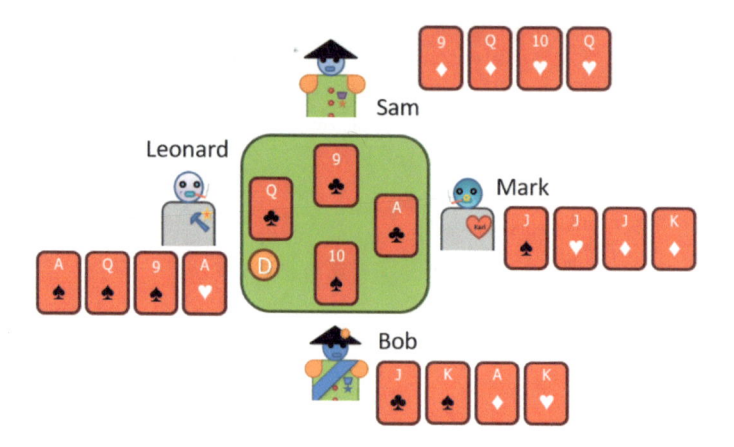

Having played the trump card, Bob takes the trick.

Commies	0
Generals	1

Bob took the trick, but Bob is not feeling well. That's because his partner didn't lead trump (which the making team would do as part of good strategy. We'll expand upon that later). So, Bob suspects that Sam doesn't have any trump cards. Bob knows that the right bower is out there somewhere (although he hopes it is buried in the kitty) and can take his left bower. And he knows that he won't be getting any trump help from his partner.

BYZANTINE GENERALS | PLAY SOME EUCHRE

Bob has the lead because he won the trick, but can't decide what to play? He could lead the left bower, playing strong, and hope for the best. He could lead the off-suit Ace and hope it goes around without getting trumped. Or he could lead the K♠ in the hopes off pulling as many trump cards out as possible, making it more likely that his off-suit Ace might survive a trick in the later rounds.

What would you do? Remember, you can't see the other cards.

Bob decides to play the K♠, attempting to draw as many trump cards as possible and saving his left bower for later.

Play looks as follows. Bob plays the K♠. Leonard tries to take the trick and decides to play his A♣. Sam throws her weakest card, the 9♦. Mark must follow suit, but takes the trick with the right bower, which is the J♠.

BYZANTINE GENERALS | PLAY SOME EUCHRE

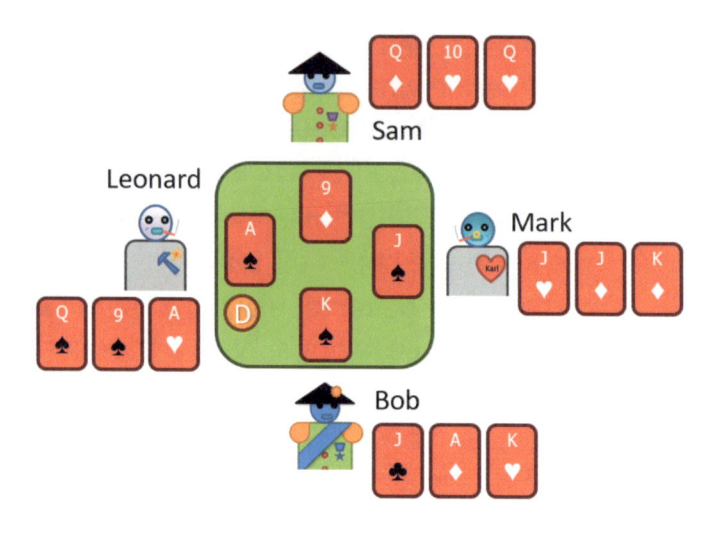

Commies	1
Generals	1

Mark won the trick and so he leads his strongest remaining card, the K♦. Bob follows suit, playing his A♦. However, Leonard doesn't have any diamonds, and trumps with his 9♠. Sam doesn't have trump or diamonds, and plays her weakest card, the 10♥. Therefore, Leonard takes this trick. The play and remaining cards are shown in the figure below.

30 | Page

BYZANTINE GENERALS | PLAY SOME EUCHRE

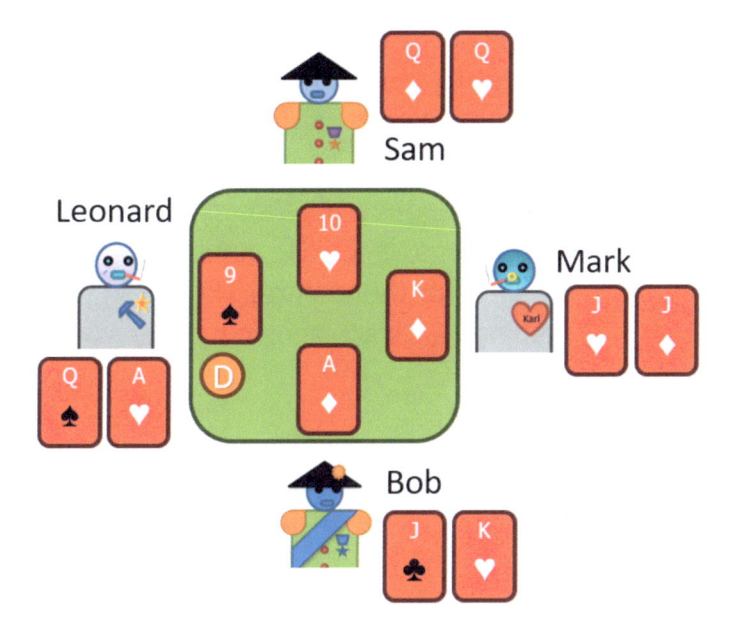

Commies	2
Generals	1

Leonard now has the lead. Because the commies didn't make trump, their overarching strategy should be to conserve their trump cards. So, Leonard will play the A♥. Sam follows suit with her queen, Mark follows suit with his jack, and Bob must follow suit with his king.

31 | Page

BYZANTINE GENERALS | PLAY SOME EUCHRE

And that's all she wrote for Bob, because with that trick the commies now have three tricks and have euchred Bob. At this point, Bob's remaining left bower doesn't matter because that would only give the generals a second trick and they need three tricks for the point. The commies get two points for the euchre. The ending play and remaining cards are shown below.

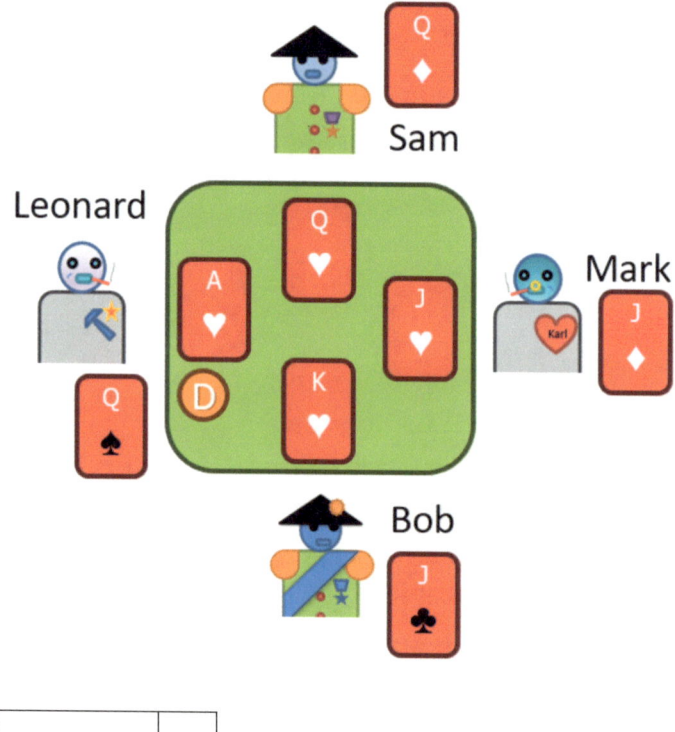

| Commies | 3 |

BYZANTINE GENERALS | PLAY SOME EUCHRE

Generals	1

Reneging and Capital Punishment

I generally support capital punishment if it is swift, and the evidence is conclusive. But, just like when we sometimes let people off with an insanity defense, I tend to cut beginners some slack when it comes to reneging. Afterall, I would like them to learn, and come back to play again, and not remember that time I berated them in front of the whole world because they made a mistake.

"What is reneging," you ask? Reneging occurs when you didn't follow the suit that was led even though you had the cards to do so. For example, a heart card was led, and you had a heart card, but you played a spade. Maybe spades were trump and you wanted to jump in there and take the trick in your excitement – forgetting that you had to follow suit.

This is sort of a judgement call. If you're a newb, you're getting a pass from me. If I've made a mistake and reneged, I will take my lumps like a man. If you're playing in a tournament – expect that no one is cutting you any slack.

However, for non-newbs if you renege - the other team gets two points. Which is the same as if your team has been euchred or if you have taken all five tricks.

Table Talk and Bluffing

Euchre isn't poker. There isn't any bluffing. You can think you see all the "tells" in the world. It doesn't matter. Why? All the cards are going to be played anyway. The cards will do the talking.

Now – you can't be telling your partner what you have in your hand either. You can't even tell them that you have a bad hand. Again, the cards will say everything that needs to be said – especially if you know how to use them to send a message.

BYZANTINE GENERALS | PLAY SOME EUCHRE

For example, this is why you want to play a bower as soon as possible. This lets your partner know where that powerful card is at. But you don't want to do that if it's going to be pulling your partner's strong trump cards.

Imagine you've taken a trick and have the lead and you're trying to decide between a weak card (9 or 10) and a medium bad card (Queen). When the Queen doesn't have a chance of taking the trick, play the weak card so that it clearly communicates to your partner they are free to take control.

Watch what your partner is playing. That might seem obvious. Because yes, it's not just about you. But I don't mean just what you partner is leading or if they're playing trump cards. Pay attention to the cards they are discarding, e.g., they can't follow suit, but they aren't playing trump cards either.

You're trying to get all five tricks? You've won three tricks, and it looks like you're going to take the fourth, if your final lead is weak, pay attention to what your partner threw away on the fourth trick – if you have two equally weak cards, play the suit your partner just threw away – they just might be throwing it away because they've

> BYZANTINE GENERALS | PLAY SOME EUCHRE

got a higher card in that same suit – if you can lead into it and your partner can take the trick – bonus!

These are examples of "letting your cards do the talking." All will be revealed in due course.

Euchre Variants That Are Stupid

There are some variants of the game out there. They are all dumb. Why do you have to be this way? For example, in some places, people play to 15, or even 21. Undoubtably, they want to drag the game out as long as possible and savor it – the opposite of "part of the joy of the game is the speed at which it's played". I like to savor the game as well – but I also like to chalk up my victories and move on with my life. The game is played to 10.

BYZANTINE GENERALS | PLAY SOME EUCHRE

No Trump

What the ever-loving... This can only be an option for people who have a hard time doing the figurin'. Yeah, if this is your favorite option, euchre probably isn't for you. You might like a game called Solitaire though.

Ace - No Face

This mode is for babies that somehow can't comprehend that even the lead is strategic and that the game is not only about bowers and Aces. If you want to play this option, put this book down right now and walk away. I'm not kidding. Put it down.

Farmer's Hand

In this option, if you have a hand that has three nines, you can exchange them for the three undealt cards in the kitty. From the school of life that says, "*Don't go with the cards you have been dealt, change the rules to accommodate your feelings*".

You may get three nine cards and you may even complement those cards with 10s. But chances are you will have a trump card in that hand, so

BYZANTINE GENERALS | PLAY SOME EUCHRE

quit yer whining. But, even if you don't, you want to slow down the game because you got one bad hand? Get out of here. Maybe your role in life is to be an example for others, have you thought of that? Everyone gets bad hands; everyone gets good hands. Take the good with the bad and move on with your life.

I will concede I could see one scenario where I would allow a Farmer's hand variant in my beloved game: If you exchange your cards with the cards in the kitty, then, if play comes to you, you must call trump just like if you were stuck. With this change you would be balancing your reward with a fair bit of risk.

BYZANTINE GENERALS | PLAY SOME EUCHRE

Terms You'll Hear

Euchre has its own language and wisdom. Often this wisdom is handed down as pithy sayings. Some are dumb. Some have merit. We'll explore a few of these. Maybe you've heard some others. Feel free to add them when you write your own book on euchre.

"You can always count on your partner".

Many players think that if you have two solid tricks that your partner will contribute one trick, giving you the requisite three. However, what happens in an actual game is that about the only thing you can count on for sure is that your partner will screw you. Have low expectations - then you're never disappointed.

Short-suited

Your hand lacks one or more of the four suits. This is generally a good thing if you've ordered, or are considering ordering trump, because it gives you a better opportunity to "trump in" because you don't have a card with which to follow what was led.

Buried

If a card was in the kitty (that you may or may not have been looking for) it may be referred to as being "buried".

Fishing For Trump

When you intentionally lead a low trump card, for example, a 9 or 10, in the hopes of pulling a bunch of the higher trump from other people's hands, such as the bowers. Or, when you know a certain suite has been played so you lead an off-suite card in the hopes of drawing a trump card out.

Kitty

The four remaining cards after dealing a new hand. Also sometimes called the "bank."

Leading back

This is a situation where your partner has led a certain suit, but you have taken the trick. Now it is your lead, so you lead the same suite back.

Why would you do this?

Because of the low number of cards in the deck, any given suite will only be played twice. Therefore, leading back will usually force a trump card to come out – hopefully your partners. Or, if you were fishing for trump, getting your opponent to play a trump card on what might be a junk card from your hand. Or, if you know that all the trump cards are out – getting a trick that no one can take because they don't have a card that can do this.

Let's look at an example.

You partner leads the Q♥, the person to your right plays the K♥, you play the A♥, and the person on your left follows suite with the 9♥. You take the trick with that Ace.

BYZANTINE GENERALS | PLAY SOME EUCHRE

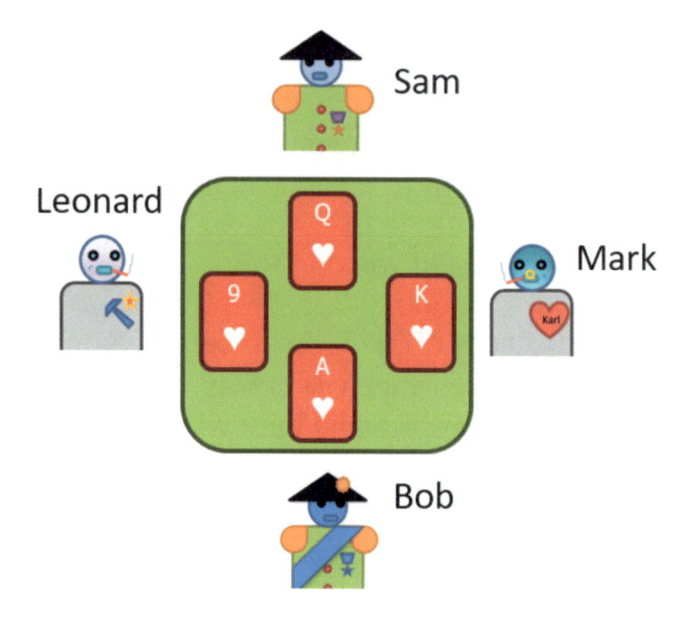

At this point you know that the only hearts that are left are the 10♥ and the J♥. If you had either one of those, then you would lead one of them back to your partner, again, to either fish out some trump, or give your partner an opportunity to take the trick (with a trump card). What will often happen if you lead one of these cards is that the person on your left will trump in, but usually use a low trump (following the conservation of power principle). This will hopefully give your partner an opportunity to over trump that card and take the trick.

Overtrump

Simply meaning that a higher trump card was played on a trump card that currently was looking like it was going to take the trick.

Protected (Left or Ace)

You have more than one trump, so if the person making trump plays the left or right bower, you have a low trump you can throw to "protect" your higher trump so that you can save it for later.

Sandbagging

A claim (usually made by weak players) when they have ordered trump, and it turns out poorly for them. Normally if someone has a good hand, they will call trump. If you happen to call trump and it was your opponent's best hand well, get better.

Sent a Boy (To do a man's job)

This remark is usually made when you have trumped a trick, but you used a low trump card and the next person playing over-trumps your card, suggesting that perhaps you should have used a higher card. Maybe you should have, maybe you shouldn't have, and maybe the card you played was intentional (because you read this

BYZANTINE GENERALS | PLAY SOME EUCHRE

book and now, you're nigh unto an expert in euchre). In any case, when this happens your opponents are likely to chide, "you sent a boy!"

Let's look at an abbreviated example. Mark has played the A♥. But in this example, spades are trump. Bob plays the 10♠. Leonard over-trumps Bob's trump with the Q♠. Leonard then attempts to besmirch Bob's good character by saying he sent a boy to do a man's job. The "job" in this case- successfully trumping Mark's Ace.

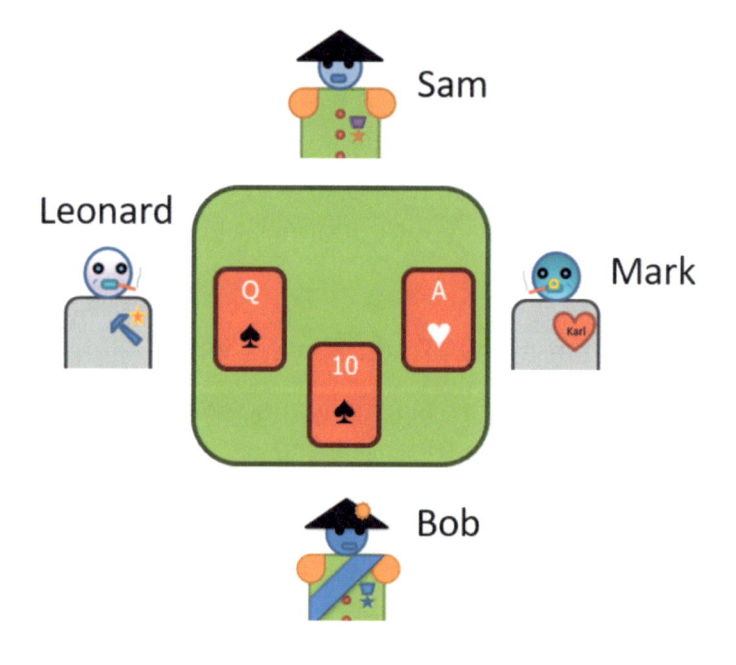

BYZANTINE GENERALS | PLAY SOME EUCHRE

Was that the case? We won't know until the hand is over. Remember the principle of conservation of power. Reserve your most powerful cards for tricks that are absolutely needed or the outcome clearer. If you're trying to draw out other trump cards without necessarily having to lead them, good on you.

The worst, most foolish way to "be a man" would be to use unnecessarily high cards to trump that Ace. For example, instead of using the 10, let's say Bob used the right bower. Well, he would certainly win the trick, but might be opening himself up to getting set if he doesn't also have strong trump cards to maintain control of the hand. If Bob played the right bower even though he had that 10, and say, the K♣, and Mark or Leonard are holding the left bower and Ace of trump, Bob is going to be in trouble.

Throwing Junk

Leading with a crap card such as a 9 or 10 that isn't trump.

Throw Off

Playing a card that is neither trump nor following suit. You can't take the trick, so you just throw one of your weaker cards.

Trump (or trumping) In

Not following suit but playing a trump card in the hopes of taking a trick.

However, there are some ways to be a good partner:

- If your partner made trump (and was not stuck) and you have the lead, lead trump. Find out why they ordered it.
- If you have a bower and your partner made trump, let them know as soon as possible. You can't come out and tell them – but play it as soon as reasonably as possible so that they know that your opponents don't have it.

BYZANTINE GENERALS | PLAY SOME EUCHRE

- Using it to take one of your opponent's tricks: Good.
- Using it to take your partner's Ace… not as good.

> I only have a low trump. But I have aces.
> Did we make trump?
> Yes.

> Do you love me?
> I'm a little iffy on that at the moment.
> Lead trump anyway.

Let's look at this example. Mark is the dealer. Your partner must have a good hand because she has ordered it up, so spades are trump. What do you lead?

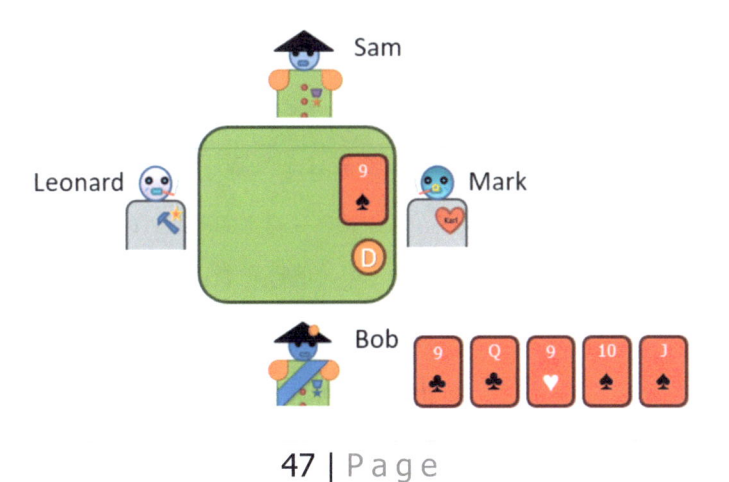

Sam

Leonard   Mark

Bob — 9♣ Q♣ 9♥ 10♠ J♠

BYZANTINE GENERALS | PLAY SOME EUCHRE

You might think, "I should lead a trump, but I want to save that bower in case we need it. I am following the principles of both "least power" and "make trump lead trump".

However, the better play is to lead the right bower. Yes, this is a power card and will pull a trump from your partner's hand, but the "least power" principle applies to the team as well. If you show your partner where the right bower is, they don't have to expend any cards to locate it. Plus, you give them the flexibility to throw away their lowest trump. If their hand was good enough to call it even though they didn't have the right bower and they ordered a trump card into the opponent's hand, you really need to be thinking about taking all five tricks, and it starts with leading the right bower.

Other ways to be a good partner:

- Let's say you have the 9, 10, Q of off-suit cards, but somehow you got the lead, and you're wondering what to play. Lead the 9. You may never get the lead again but send a clear signal to your partner that the trick is theirs to take. That Queen isn't going

BYZANTINE GENERALS | PLAY SOME EUCHRE

around anyway (unless of course, you know that the Ace/King have been accounted for and there is not anymore trump, then, lead the Queen).

- Leading back – we defined this earlier. If you've taken a trick but need to pass control back to your partner, lead back the same suit that was just played. Since it has already been played, this should give them an opportunity to use trump. Why? If a suit has already been played, as many as four of the six cards of that suit will get pulled. If four came out, it means that if you can lead that same suit back, there is only one other card of that suit. It will force people to play trump or to throw off.
- Shorting yourself (reducing the number of suits in your hand) when your partner orders trump. Consider the figure below. You're the dealer with the 10♦ showing.

BYZANTINE GENERALS | PLAY SOME EUCHRE

Your partner orders that diamond – so, which of your cards do you discard?

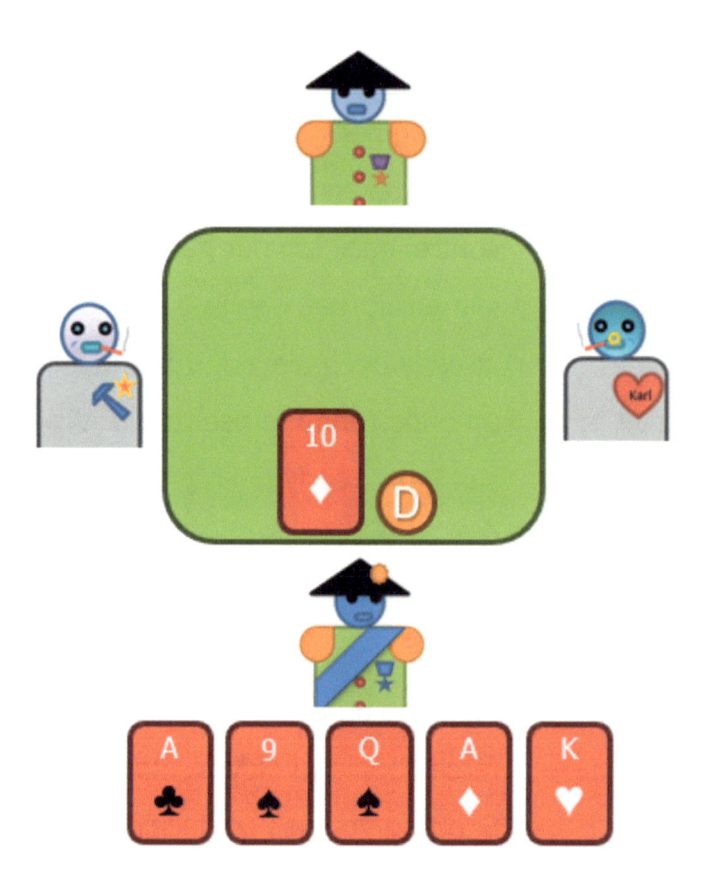

You don't want to discard either of your diamonds because diamonds are now trump. You don't want to discard that off-suit Ace, even though it would short suit you in spades because, it is an

BYZANTINE GENERALS | PLAY SOME EUCHRE

Ace. If you discard a spade, it still leaves you with one spade so that isn't an option. The correct answer is that you discard the K♥, even though the King is a higher card than either the 9♠ or Q♠. Why do you want to be short-suited? Because this will maximize your opportunity to trump in – otherwise you will almost always be forced to follow suit. The chance to trump in and take a trick is of greater value than holding onto a card that likely won't take a trick. Now if that King was instead an Ace, again, you would hold onto the Ace and then discard one of your spades. Although not leaving you short-suited, an Ace has a greater chance of taking a trick.

It's little things like these which essentially give your partner clues through your playing, that help (or should) them with their situational awareness as to what cards are still out there waiting to pounce.

Stupid Things You'll Hear

"Wow. I have a *really* good poker hand".

Of course, you do. *Half of the cards were removed from the deck which limits the variability*

BYZANTINE GENERALS | PLAY SOME EUCHRE

and most of what remains are face cards. Please stop talking.

Principles (Not Rules)

In this section we'll talk about guidelines and principles that reflect good strategy and being a good partner.

Principle: Conservation of power

The goal is to win a trick, thereby the hand, and then, the game. But not just to win a hand – but to win it by expending the least amount of power possible. If you can play a nine, off-suit card, and it gets trumped – that is a good outcome because the other team had to expend power to get control. If you play an off-suit nine and it goes around (for example, it's the last trick of the hand and no one has cards of that suit remaining) and takes the trick – you are a euchre master (or lucky).

Principle: Part of the joy of the game

Is the speed at which it is played.

This is why I advocate for not cutting the deck on the deal and why playing with the "stick the dealer" option is a must.

Other "speed" options include things such as, a situation where you have the two highest cards (both bowers). If you do, just lay them down and let each person discard two cards. *Forward! Forward to victory!* Or, if you have the highest card remaining that can keep the other team from getting all the tricks (the "stopper") – just say you have the stopper and throw it in. People will respect your respect for the principle.

Now – keep in mind, if you *don't* have the cards that you think you do, be prepared to give the other team two points because you reneged. Also, remember, you've been looking at your cards all hand, don't throw down and immediately scoop up – give the other players a second to just confirm that, yep, it is as you say. In fact, if you make the play, don't scoop at all – let the other team do it once the painful realization has set in that they have been foiled.

Principle: If your team didn't order trump

Then don't lead trump.

But if you lead trump, you pull it out of your opponent's hands, right? Yes, that's true. But you also pull it out of your *partner's* hand. Even if you have the right bower (and unless you're sitting on three trump cards), let the flow of play come to you. If your partner has a trump card, give them a chance to play it. You take that chance away if you pull it out of their hand when you're defending.

Principle: If You Can Take a Trick – Do It

The only exception to this principle is obviously when you shouldn't.

So confusing!

Yes, I know. This is one of those situations that you will get a better understanding of when you get a feel for the game. And sometimes, this involves learning to let go.

BYZANTINE GENERALS | PLAY SOME EUCHRE

You already know that you don't trump your partner's Ace (except when you need to take control). But conversely, sometimes, especially if you have a weak hand or the taking of the trick is otherwise in question, maybe throw off and see if your partner can take the trick. For example, let's look at the situation below. You've bravely called spades trump based on the three that you have and an off-suit Ace. A decent hand but with the bowers and the Ace of trump still out there, a little partner help would, well, help.

BYZANTINE GENERALS | PLAY SOME EUCHRE

Mark has led the Q♥. Now, you could take it with one of your trump cards. But that off-suit queen isn't particularly strong. This is an opportunity to let go and see if you partner has the K♥ or A♥, or even better, one of those bowers that you're looking for.

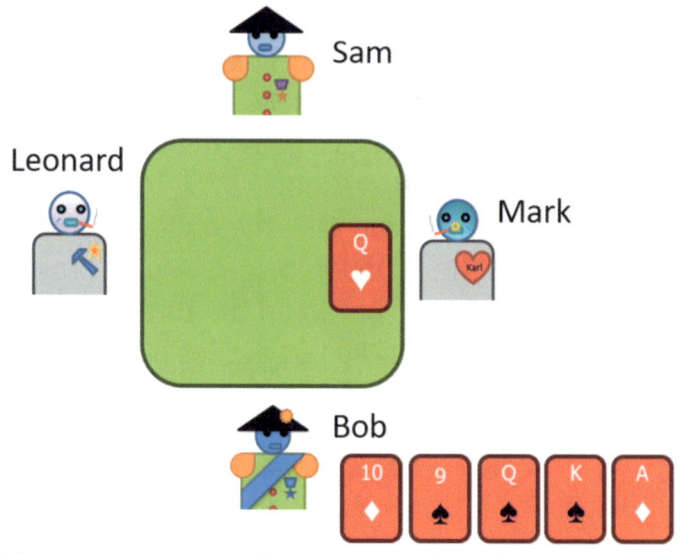

Playing your low off-suit card, the 10, lets you burn a trick and see if your partner can take it. You still have your off-suit Ace and those three trump cards in case that play doesn't work out. This follows the conservation of power principle that we discussed earlier.

BYZANTINE GENERALS | PLAY SOME EUCHRE

Principle: Secure Your Point First

Then go for two.

It is tempting when you have a mittful of trump to just start laying those things like crazy. Be mindful of weak spots in your hand. Make sure you have those three tricks secured – and then once you know they are in the bag, *only then* do you go for the last two.

Did that last trump card that could take yours get played? Or are you counting on it being in the kitty or your partner's hand? Maybe go fishing for trump (and giving up a trick) to make sure. Better to only get one point, than getting euchred and giving the other team two.

Principle: If You Make Trump – Lead Trump

And the converse – principle: If your team didn't order trump, then don't lead it.

First – the why behind the principles, then we'll address the exceptions.

Nominally, if your team called trump, then you're the ones in position of power – you called it on *something*, right? Also, because you want to dictate the flow of the game. So, if you ordered

BYZANTINE GENERALS | PLAY SOME EUCHRE

the trump, lead it. You want to pull out the opposing team's trump cards, and then polish them off with your Ace(s). Keeping in mind – once the trump cards are off the table then this makes the Aces good, as in, they can't be trumped. As a result, they revert to their normal lofty power status.

This principle even holds if you don't have any of the bowers. Lead your trump. Doing so either pulls those bowers out of your opponent's hands so that they can't trump your tricks later; or leads into your partner's bowers. Either way, it's a good move.

The "Stuck" Exception

What is the exception to the "make it, lead it" principle? When you or your partner (especially your partner) orders trump because one of you have been stuck. If you've been stuck – you're the dealer, so you're at the mercy of whatever gets led.

If you're stuck, then the person to your left has the lead. If your partner takes that trick, *they should not lead trump back*; unless of course, they want to control the rest of the hand. Which shouldn't be the case – otherwise they would have ordered it in the first place.

Why? Because if you get stuck, by definition, you usually have a weak hand. If they lead trump, they might pull trump from the opponents, but they also pull trump from you; and it's likely you don't have many. It is better to let the person that was stuck determine when they want to play (and lead) their trump if they so desire.

Strategy

In this section various scenarios that you'll encounter while playing will be explored – with some advice on how to navigate them.

The core of euchre strategy is "play your strong cards and get rid of your weak cards".

Yep - That's it. Everything else is nuance.

But it turns out – euchre is full of nuance. Let's dig into more nuanced ways in which to achieve victory.

First, think about, what is your path to victory? Are you making trump, supporting your partner, or defending. A glance at your cards will usually indicate where you're going to land. If you are making trump, are you leading strong, or do you have a weak hand and need some help? Knowing if you're going to fish for trump, get the lead, or throw off. Knowing when to throw "junk cards" is as much about getting to winning a trick as leading trump is. Let's dig into some of these options.

Should I call Trump?

Here are some principles (not rules) regarding the calling of trump.

I personally like to use a hand strength system. For each potential trump card in my hand, I give myself a point, for each non-trump Ace (also referred to as "off-suit"), I give myself half a point. As a general guideline, my threshold for calling trump is to have a hand strength of three. If the dealer has turned down trump and I can call it anything I want, I will sometimes go with a 2.5-point guideline – depending on how strong my potential trump would be and how strong my off-suit cards are.

Are you short-suited? This is another guideline. If all four suits are present in your hand – generally

BYZANTINE GENERALS | PLAY SOME EUCHRE

don't call trump unless you have a couple high trump cards and an off-suit Ace.

What will often happen when you have all four suits in your hand is that you will end up following suit during the hand being played and will rarely get a chance to dictate the terms of play with your trump. Or if you do, it will be short-lived. You usually want to be at least short suited in one suit, ideally two. This is the "three trump, two suit" guideline. If you have such a hand this is usually a safe (but not guaranteed) path to a point.

Let's look at an "all four suits" example where I "might" be able to squeak by because I have a couple decent trump cards.

This might work as my partner is the dealer and a high trump is showing, the A♠. I've got the right bower and the queen if I order spades.

BYZANTINE GENERALS | PLAY SOME EUCHRE

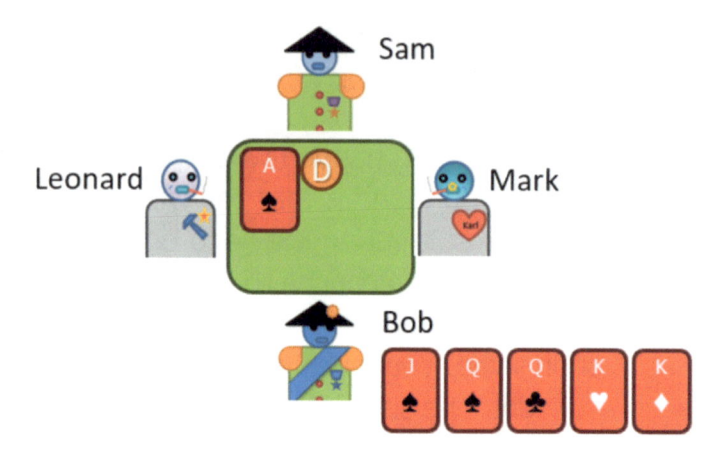

Let's give it a go and see what happens.

Mark has the lead and plays the K♣. Bob must follow suit with Q♣. Leonard plays the A♣, and Sam must also follow suit and plays the 9♣, so Leonard takes the trick.

Commies	1
Generals	0

Leonard leads with the 9♦ (he must have a weak hand over there). Bob's partner Sam must not have diamonds because she plays the 10♠, trumping in. Mark follows suit with the J♦, and

62 | Page

BYZANTINE GENERALS | PLAY SOME EUCHRE

Bob follows suit with the K♦ so my partner Sam takes the trick.

Commies	1
Generals	1

Since Bob ordered spades, Sam decides to play the A♠ to find out why. Mark follows suit with the K♠. Now, Bob knows the left bower is still out there so plays the right bower because he knows he should take it if he can. Leonard plays the left bower, so Bob takes the trick.

Commies	1
Generals	2

That last trick pulled out all the good trump, so Bob leads the highest one left, the Q♠. Leonard plays the 10♦, my partner plays the 9♥, Mark plays the 10♥, and the generals have secured the point with that third trick.

BYZANTINE GENERALS | PLAY SOME EUCHRE

Commies	1
Generals	3

The Generals take three tricks on a hand that had a lot of risk associated with calling it because Bob was four-suited with no off-suit Aces. But this was an occasion where Bob's partner Sam, came through with not just the trump card that was showing (the Ace) but an extra one that she could play because while Bob wasn't short-suited, she was.

The Generals won that hand because Bob's partner Sam, unbeknownst to him, had two trump and was short-suited (no diamonds). As such, she had an opportunity to trump in, and most importantly, led back trump to give Bob a chance to take a trick with the right bower.

Which just goes to show, if you're going to make a sketchy call, it's good to have a partner to back you up. If Sam is *not* short-suited, or if Bob has the left bower instead of the right bower, that hand likely ends up with two points for the commies.

Should I go Alone?

Are you brave? Going alone can be scary. But it doesn't have to be. Sometimes the call is a no-brainer - a lay-down. You were dealt five trump cards including one of the bowers? Go alone.

Keep in mind – you don't necessarily need to have the right bower in your hand to go alone. Any given card could be in your partner's hand or in the kitty. It's almost an equal bet. Your partner and the kitty have nine cards, all told. Your opponents have ten, all told. That's a 45% chance the card you're looking for is buried. And of course, a 55% chance that it is lurking out there waiting for you to make a mistake.

It's a stretch, but say you have the Q, K, and A of trump, are two-suited, with one of those off-suit cards being an Ace, I might be tempted to go alone Yes, I would be betting that *both* bowers are buried. Right-that's why I said it was a stretch. But, even if both bowers are in one person's hand, and that person is your opponent, it's true those two bowers would take two of your trump cards. But they would also take *all other trump*, leaving you with a trump and an Ace to control three other tricks.

BYZANTINE GENERALS | PLAY SOME EUCHRE

In that scenario, you still get a point and would be unlikely to be euchred (and then become infamous for not bringing your partner along when they might have helped you pick up a couple tricks).

Can I go alone if I am three-suited? If you have strong trump cards and at least one off-suit Ace, then yes, you can go alone. For example, if hearts are trump and your hand looks like:

J♥, J♦, Q♥, A♣, Q♠

This is a strong hand. The two bowers guarantee that you get two tricks. If the opposing team leads a ♣ you can take the trick with your Ace. If they lead a ♦ you can trump it with your queen of trump. The only weak spot is the Q♠. If the opposing team leads a ♠ your loner will be over before it starts. With this hand you're hoping that the off-suit queen can make it until the last trick and hope that the king and Ace of spades is buried or has already been played.

Should you bring your partner along for that hand?

BYZANTINE GENERALS | PLAY SOME EUCHRE

That is always the question: Do I bring my partner and get two points, or do I go alone for a shot at four points?

Keep in mind, there is no guarantee that your partner will have the King or Ace of Spades. And there's no guarantee that even if they did, it wouldn't get trumped. These are long odds, however. I like to live dangerously. I'm going alone.

Consider the following four-trump scenarios. When should you bring your partner along?

If you have four trump and your fifth card is:

- Ace – I will go alone 100% of the time.
- King – I will go alone 100% of the time.
- Queen – I will go alone 100% of the time.
- Ten – I will go alone ~50% of the time.
- Nine – I will almost never go alone.

Why do I waver when it comes to the nine and ten cards?

There are just too many cards out there lurking. If your fifth card is the 10, there are four higher cards in that suit that can win the trick. And there are four places it could be – two of those places

BYZANTINE GENERALS | PLAY SOME EUCHRE

being your opponent's hands. If you have the nine, then there are five cards that can take your card and it's likely that someone might have two chances to take your card.

And keep in mind, as you progress through a hand, people are getting rid of their weakest cards. And they will be following suit or getting their trump cards pulled or played – leaving... something that is going to beat your 9 or 10.

Stopping a Loner Hand

Beating a loner hand is rare. But it can happen. If the Sun is sitting just right and you're say, eating a peanut butter and jelly sandwich outside of the laundromat in Waterton, Canada, it can be possible.

But let's focus on getting that loner stopped and limiting the other team to a single point.

> Loners, if they can be stopped, are usually stopped on the first or last trick.

Loners are usually stopped on the first or last trick. And I should clarify, if you're holding the right bower when someone on the other team went alone, yes, that is a no brainer. For all other cases – let's walk through some of the opportunities that might present themselves.

Usually, the person going alone will have a mitt full of trump cards – and these usually come out in the midst of the hand. If you have the lead, the first trick is where you might have an opportunity to find the hole in their hand.

Otherwise, if the person going alone doesn't have five trump cards, they may be out of trump and have been saving their weakest card for last in the hopes that you can't follow suit (See the list of fifth card options above). If you've saved the correct suit, this is usually your other opportunity to stop their loner.

Thus, your chances of stopping a loner will depend on the type of loner you're defending from. If your opponent has five trump cards, unless you have a protected left or the right bower, you can forget it. What we're after here are loners that might have a weak spot.

Let's discuss the situation where the person going alone has four trump cards and one off-suit card. If the off-suit card (in a four-trump card hand) is not an Ace – you have an opening, albeit small.

BYZANTINE GENERALS | PLAY SOME EUCHRE

Some tactics for stopping the loner:

- "Protected left (or Ace)"- That is, your opponent has the right bower, but you have the left bower or Ace of trump that is protected by a lower trump card. Sit on those trump cards until you absolutely need to play them. Let your opponent come out with their right bower, get rid of your lower trump card, and save the left bower/Ace to take a trick later in the hand.
- Some opportunities are based on where you are sitting relative to the person going along.
    - Suppose the person going alone is on your left and your partner has the lead. If they lead anything besides an Ace and you have a trump card, trump it.

- o If the person going alone is on your right and your partner has the lead, wait to see what the person going alone does – do they trump in? Can you over trump?
- Choices when you have the lead (these look just like your options during a normal hand):
  - o If you have an Ace – lead that card.
  - o If you have several cards of the same suit, lead one of them. Yes, the chances are that the person going alone will be short that suit (because you have most of them) – but this also gives your partner a chance to play a trump card because they will also likely be short that suit. Suppose your partner is short the suit you play, and the person going alone must follow suit – now your partner can play a trump card if they have

one and – *ta da!* You've stopped the loaner.

- If all else fails, I will lead a suit in the same color of the suit in which the person going alone has chosen. For example, if they are going alone in hearts, I will lead a diamond. Why? It is less likely that a person will have all five black or all five red cards in their hand (Unlikely, but not zero). If I don't have a strong card to open with, then I want to set up a chance to stop on the last trick. Thus, I want to narrow down what suit the final card will be. I usually start by eliminating the "all red" or "all black" situation and go from there. Eliminating this option will usually give me more cards to "throw away" as they are playing their trump so I can increase my chances of picking the correct suit as the last card.

- Your other chance might be in a situation where the person going alone has the classic three trump card, two suit hand – they just happen to be going alone because they think it's a strong hand. Keep an eye on what off-suit cards (if any) that they play. If they play an off-suit card, and you have an extra card of that suit that you can save – save it in case it comes up again on the last trick.

You're Stuck – Now What?

You are of course, playing with the "stick the dealer" option – because you are smart, brave, and probably good-looking.

> BYZANTINE GENERALS | PLAY SOME EUCHRE

But it happens, now and again that sword will swing your way and you're stuck and faced with calling something with a less than ideal hand. If your hand was great, you might have called it already. In truth, your hand likely stinks. It's rare when the call has gone around the table *twice* waiting for your perfect call. That doesn't happen.

Your hand likely ranges from bad to awful.

But take heart, euchre warrior – there may be hope. Afterall – if anyone else had a great hand, they would have called it by now as well. Of course, your hand may be truly awful; so, you call what you can, lose and move on. My research has shown that roughly 70% of stuck hands are successful.

Why? Because 1) – as I said, everyone's hand is awful, and 2) you need to recognize what your best option is looking at the cards in front of you.

Let's consider this middling scenario.

Bob is "stuck" with the Ace♣ and 9♣, the 10♥ and Q♥, and the 10♠ of spades. Diamonds, of which he has none, have already been passed on by everyone.

BYZANTINE GENERALS | PLAY SOME EUCHRE

Bob has some options here. He has that Ace – and he is short suited (no diamonds).

Looking at that Ace♣ and 9♣ of clubs, that would give Bob two trump cards, so he calls that, right?

Wrong.

Following the hand strength principle, if he called hearts, that would also give him two trump cards (2 strength), but then he also has the off-suit Ace in reserve (.5 hand strength point); following the hand strength principle, this gives Bob 2.5 points.

One other thing to consider is that since diamonds were turned down, it could be that one or more of the red bowers is buried. Thus, calling hearts is going "next".

Hey, I said, "it could be." Bob is clinging to hope here. The alternative is that this is the one time one needs to count on our partner for one and hope that they have a bower.

BYZANTINE GENERALS | PLAY SOME EUCHRE

> **I have a bad hand, but I'm clinging to hope.**
>
> **Well, we're going to put an end to that.**
>
> **THERE'S NO PLACE LIKE CAMP**

Bob is the dealer so the person to his left (Leonard) leads the A♠. Sam follows with the Q♠, Mark also follows with the 9♠, and Bob plays the 10♠.

Commies	1
Generals	0

Good news, Bob is now short-suited in two suits. Also, since Leonard didn't come after Bob with trump, it may be that he is also weak in trump.

Leonard now leads the Q♦, our partner trumps in with the K♥ (*yay partner – you took your one*

BYZANTINE GENERALS | PLAY SOME EUCHRE

trick!). And Mark follows suit with the K♦. Bob can now throw away the 9♣, preserving the two trump and Ace of clubs.

Commies	1
Generals	1

Sam now leads the K♣. Is she fishing for trump? Is she hoping that Bob has the Ace that won't get trumped by Leonard? Sam is not leading trump (which you would normally do when you make trump) because this is a stuck hand. More than likely Sam suspects that Bob is weak in trump and doesn't want to pull them out unnecessarily.

Bob must play the A♣ to follow suit, and Leonard also follows with the 10♣.

Commies	1
Generals	2

Bob now has two cards, and two trump left, and the lead. Time to go fishing!

Bob leads the 10♥.

Oh glory, it works. Leonard plays his 9♥ that he was clinging to, and Sam, plays the A♥ that she was also saving, and Mark plays the big dog, the right bower (J♥), taking the trick. But Bob has done the job. By successfully going fishing for trump, now five out of the seven trump cards have been played and Bob is holding one of the remaining two. Unfortunately, the other remaining trump is the left bower – but it is likely buried or else it would have been played already.

| Commies | 2 |
| Generals | 2 |

Sure enough, Mark leads the 10♦, Bob plays his last trump (Q♥), Leonard plays the 9♦, and Sam plays the Q♣.

| Commies | 2 |
| Generals | 3 |

BYZANTINE GENERALS | PLAY SOME EUCHRE

And Bob has successfully navigated being stuck.

It obviously won't always go your way. Sure, research indicates that 70% of the time you can be successful when being stuck, but that leaves a 30% chance of losing the hand. But here's the thing – everyone is going to get stuck eventually. These things have a way of working themselves out. But understanding your situational awareness (as was demonstrated in this walkthrough) can help you be successful more often than not.

When Three Points Is a Trap!

Recall how in the section on "Should I Call Trump?" we looked at the hand strength principle regarding when to order trump. Here, we will look at how that can go awry. What otherwise might *look* like a good hand, is really a trap.

The situation:

BYZANTINE GENERALS | PLAY SOME EUCHRE

Your Seat: Left of the dealer

Showing: A ♣.

Your hand: J♠, K♣ and Q♣, Q♠, and 10♦.

BYZANTINE GENERALS | PLAY SOME EUCHRE

Nominally, you have a hand strength of three, and you're short-suited as you have no hearts. But, if the right bower is not buried, or it is in your partner's hand, you will likely lose this hand if you order it up.

This is because if the dealer's A♣ is protected, their remaining trump will be higher than any of your remaining trump, and you have no off-suite Ace to fall back on. Although, since you are short-suited with this hand, if hearts are played, you potentially have a way to take a trick with a low trump.

Let's order this and see how it plays out.

Since I made trump, I can come out strong with my trump, or I can throw junk and hope my partner can grab that trick.

I lead the left bower, my partner has the right, and plays it, thus, I suspect it is likely their only trump. Both bowers are now out of the game – so that part is good.

BYZANTINE GENERALS | PLAY SOME EUCHRE

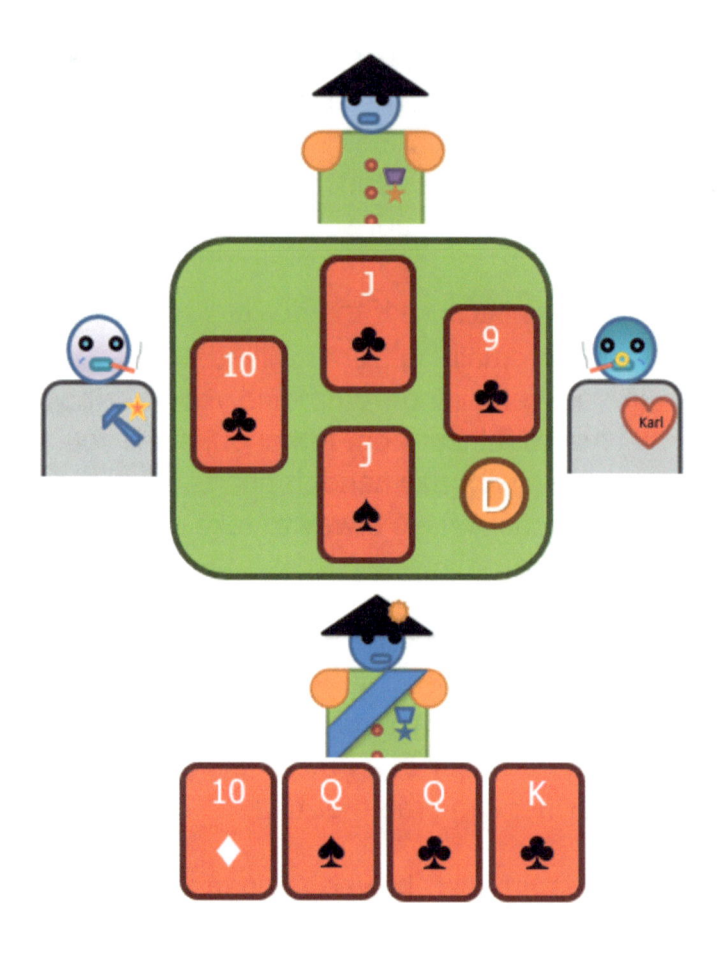

Unfortunately, the dealer (who holds the A♣ that we ordered) throws the 9♣, thus that A♣ is protected and is now the highest trump remaining.

BYZANTINE GENERALS | PLAY SOME EUCHRE

| Commies | 0 |
| Generals | 1 |

My partner (who took the trick with the right bower) now leads the K♥. The dealer throws the Q♦. I could throw off. It's always iffy with the King lead. There is usually an Ace waiting for it. Since the dealer threw off and you have no hearts, it's likely that the person to your left has the Ace – so this would be a good time to trump in.

We play our Q♣ to trump in. The person to our left throws in the 10♥. They may still have the Ace but decided to hold it since they don't have a higher trump card than what I played.

BYZANTINE GENERALS | PLAY SOME EUCHRE

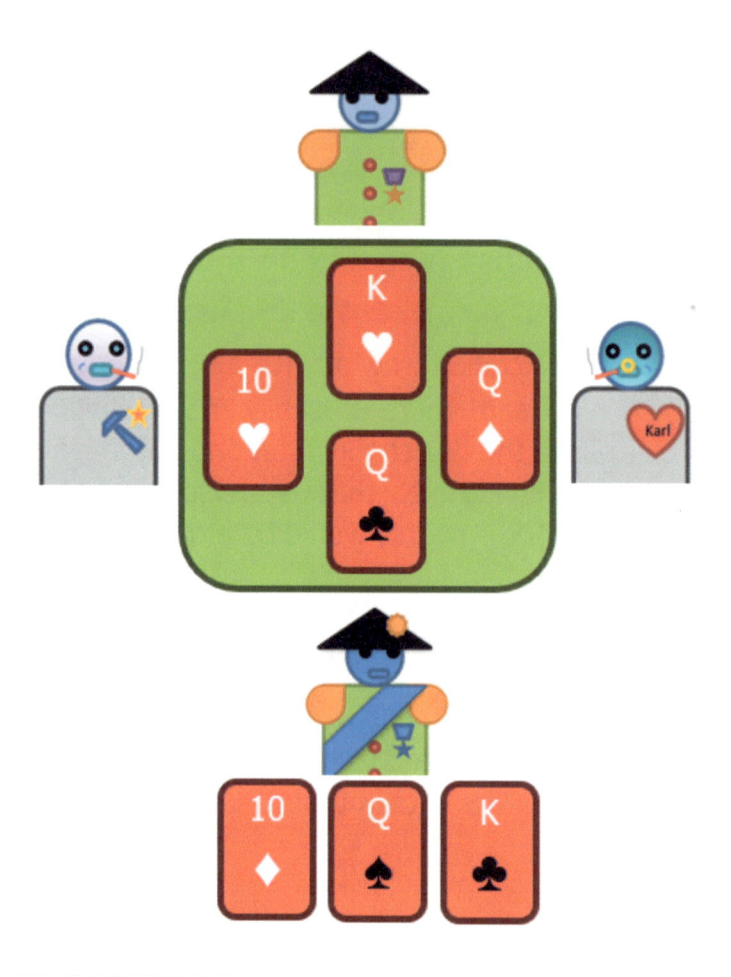

Commies	0
Generals	2

84 | Page

BYZANTINE GENERALS | PLAY SOME EUCHRE

Now what do you do? We're close – we only need one more trick! Alas, you can't lead your K♣ because the dealer's Ace would take it. You don't want to lead your 10♦ because the dealer has also played diamonds so they may have another one. Spades have not been played yet so we lead the Queen in the hopes that your partner can take it or you're going fishing for trump in the hopes that the dealer plays their Ace of trump.

Boo – we play the Q♠, everyone has a spade (since they had not been played yet this was likely), and the dealer has the A♠ taking the trick.

BYZANTINE GENERALS | PLAY SOME EUCHRE

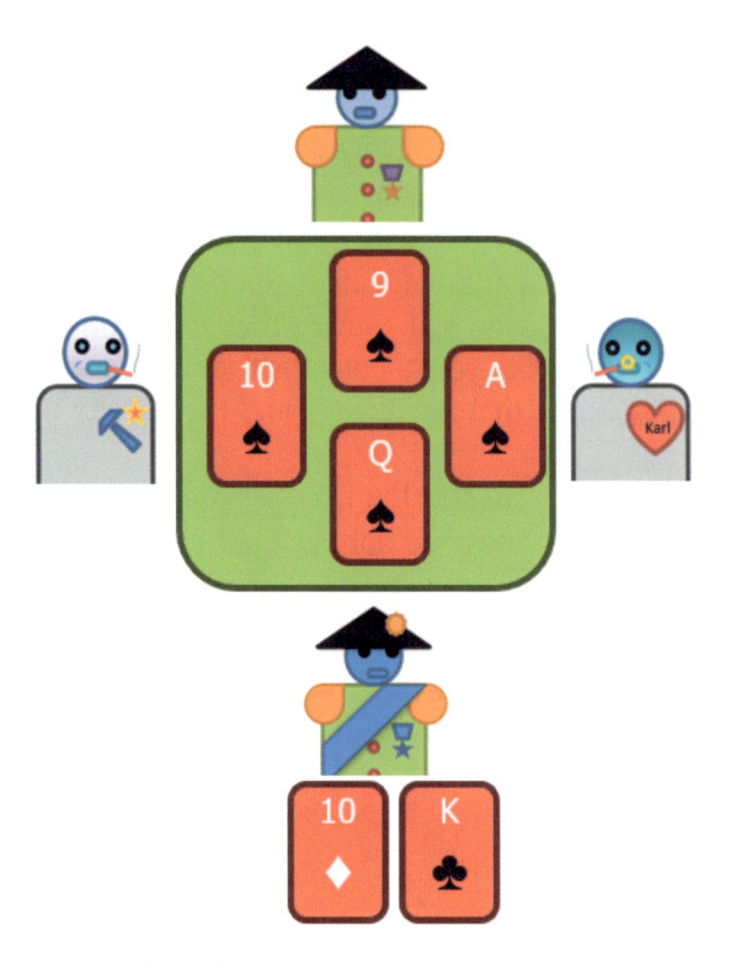

Commies	1
Generals	2

BYZANTINE GENERALS | PLAY SOME EUCHRE

Knowing they have the highest remaining trump, they lead their A♣, pulling our K♣. Their partner and yours both throw hearts (Ace and Nine respectively).

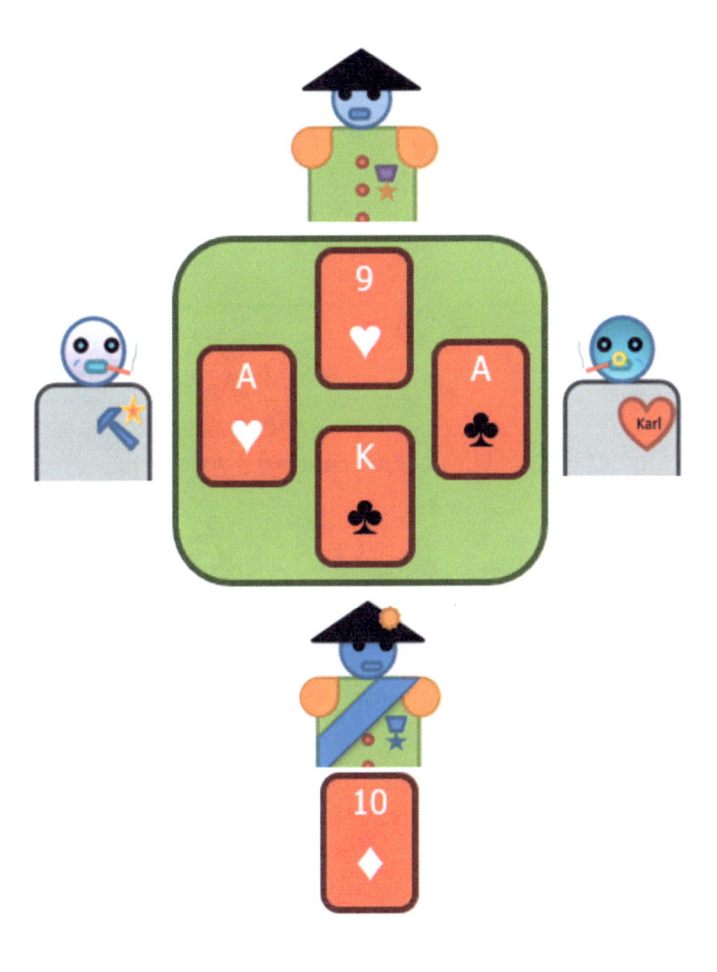

BYZANTINE GENERALS | PLAY SOME EUCHRE

Commies	2
Generals	2

And the dealer now leads their last card, as we suspected, a diamond. It just so happens to be the Ace, taking our Ten. There are no more trump cards remaining so our partner can't save us.

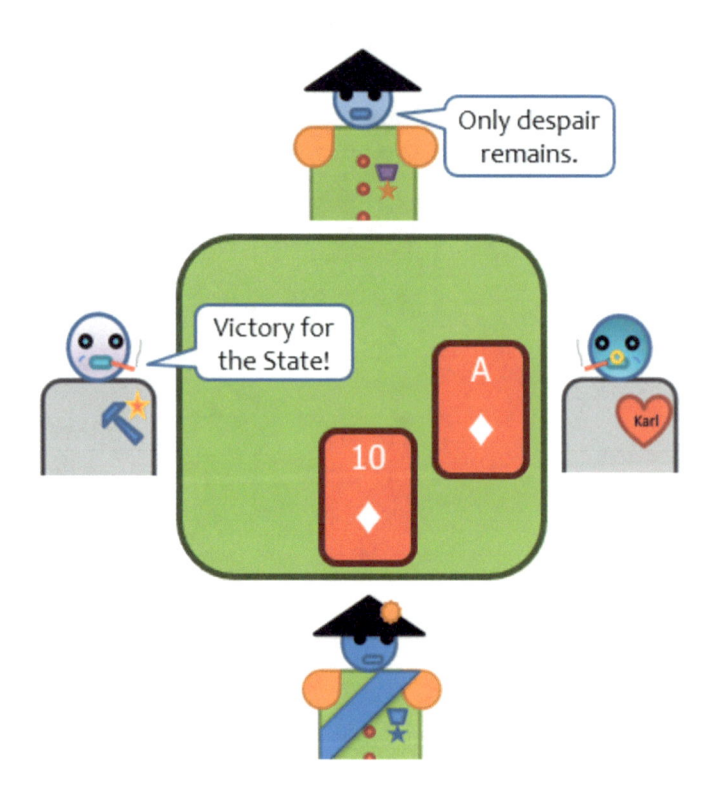

> Only despair remains.

> Victory for the State!

BYZANTINE GENERALS | PLAY SOME EUCHRE

Commies	3
Generals	2

Thus, we see how what might appear to be a strong hand (three trump, short-suited), even when our partner has the right bower, loses to a hand with only two trump and two Aces (notice that the dealer also meets the hand strength "three-point principle").

Even if we had done the "throw junk" option to start this hand, the dealers hand matches too closely, and they will protect their trump. If we lead with our 10♦, they can take it with their off-suite, and then lead an off-suite Ace that everyone follows. When you can finally trump in, you lead the left bower to get at that A♣ they're holding. But, it's protected, so you only manage to pull your partner's right bower along with their baby trump. The only way to win would be to somehow read your partner's mind and know that they have the right, so that you would lead your K♣, knowing the Ace is waiting for you.

BYZANTINE GENERALS | PLAY SOME EUCHRE

Best plan – it may look like it hurts, but pass. However, if you get a similar hand, but with an off-suit Ace to help, then call it.

Securing That Last Trick

This one is super easy. Watch the card that your partner plays the trick before.

Should I order the opponent's right bower?

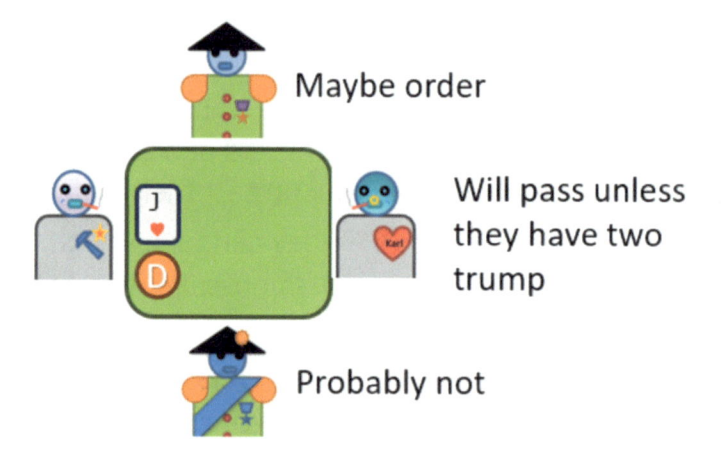

Maybe order

Will pass unless they have two trump

Probably not

Consider this scenario from the figure above:

To have any chance of success with this, you need to be in a situation where you can control the flow of the hand. You also need to hope that the person whose hand you order the right bower into isn't holding a bunch of other trump cards. If

BYZANTINE GENERALS | PLAY SOME EUCHRE

you have three trump cards, and you're looking at the fourth (the right bower that you're considering ordering up) it's pretty even odds the other three trump cards will be split among the other three hands (your partner, the other opponent, and the kitty).

But ideally, you need the lead so you can dictate play. If you don't have the lead you need to keep in mind that you'll likely need one trump to get the lead, and then another trump to go "fishing" for that right bower. Thus, if you don't have the lead you might want to let this one go because it could be a "trap" hand (A hand that otherwise looks great but one that will get you euchred – see the earlier scenario).

Let's look at a tempting scenario:

You're holding the 10♥, Q♥, and K♥, but also you are two-suited with the A♠ and the K♠. And you have the lead (The "Maybe Order" position above).

BYZANTINE GENERALS | PLAY SOME EUCHRE

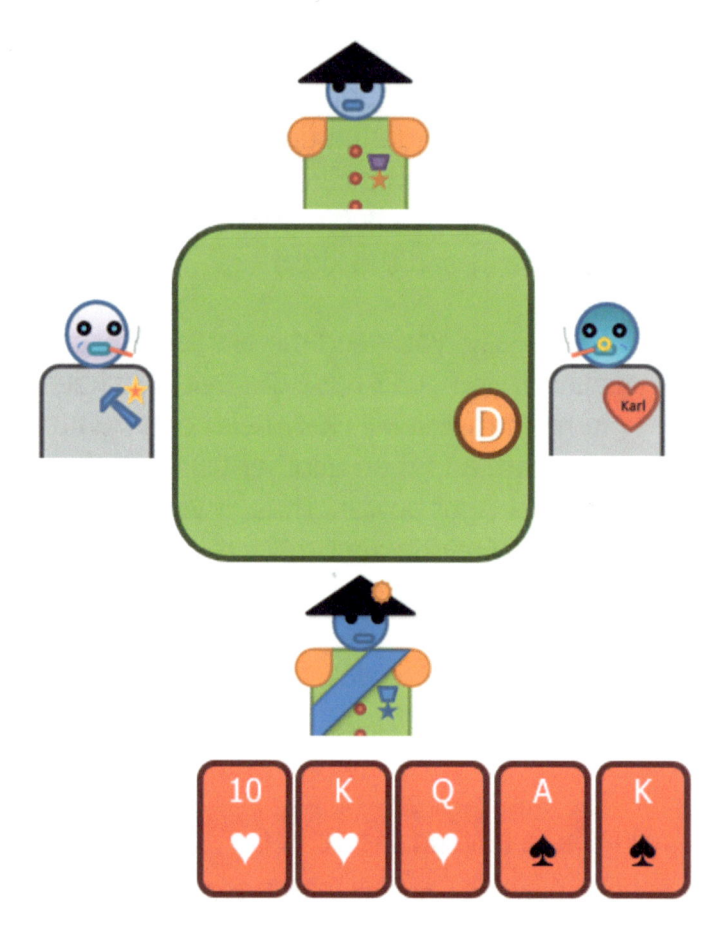

What you want to do is "go fishing for trump." Lead your lowest trump. This will require the others to follow suit if they have trump.

How is this for a worst-case scenario. You lead that 10♥, but only pull the left bower and the

BYZANTINE GENERALS | PLAY SOME EUCHRE

Ace, and your partner had no trump. That means the right bower is still out there! It's over! (No, it's not).

Smelling weakness, suppose the dealer (Leonard, who took that trick with the left bower) and comes after you with the right bower (I know I would).

You must follow suit, but throw your weakest trump, which is now the Q♥. That leaves you with the K♥, and your off-suit Ace.

The dealer, who now has the lead courtesy of taking the trick with the right bower, leads their own Ace. No doubt thinking that victory is at hand.

This is when you trump with the K♥, taking that trick. Now you lead your own Ace. The only card you need worry about is the 9♥. If the dealer has it, you lose. If your partner or Mark had that card, it would have already been played in the earlier tricks.

Voila! The other team not only had the right bower but had the three highest trump cards, yet you still took the hand. But, this is a situation where if you have three trump cards, are two-suited, and *importantly*, have the lead, that can be enough for the point.

If you don't have the lead, unless your opponent leads into your off-suit Ace, you would likely need to burn a trump card to get control which would leave you in a very weak position. This difference of having the lead versus not having the lead is the difference between your team getting a point and the other team getting two. Choose wisely!

Should I order my partner's bower?

"They say" never order your partner's right bower when it is showing. Well obviously, if you don't have any cards of that suit, best pass and let your partner be the judge of what they have.

But when do I order that right bower?

Usually, it's when I would have ordered it anyway – when something has met that 2.5 – 3 hand strength guidelines for calling trump. If you have two trump and an Ace, or three trump – chances are the other trump cards are spread across four hands (your partners, two opponents, and the kitty). It could likely be that the right bower that

BYZANTINE GENERALS | PLAY SOME EUCHRE

is showing for your partner would be the only trump that they would have.

In this case, order it but, play the hand like that card is their only trump. A good approach is to see if you can give your partner a chance to use it at minimal cost to you in terms of the strength of the cards in your hand. For example, by leading a low trump cards as soon as possible.

It can be a bad feeling when your partner turns over a right bower that you didn't order when that could have been an easy 1-point hand.

When Should I Throw That Ace Away

That Ace in your hand. It sure is tempting to hold onto it. Afterall, it's an Ace – maybe not trump, but surely a good card. But are there times when I should get rid of it?

BYZANTINE GENERALS | PLAY SOME EUCHRE

Yes, there are two times you should throw away your ace: 1) when you'll never have the lead again; and 2) when you could.

Well, thank goodness that's not confusing at all.

Let's look at the first situation – when you'll never have the lead again. This is when you don't currently have the lead, and you don't have any trump in which to grab the lead. Play comes to your hand, and you can't play a trump card and you need to throw something away.

If the suit in which you hold the Ace has already been played, and if your remaining cards include suits that haven't been played yet (assuming there's no Ace in there with which you can get the lead), your best bet might be to ditch the Ace and hope for the best.

The other situation is when you have an Ace – but you also have a trump card, and your partner has the current trick in hand (meaning – it looks like your partner will take it). Your best play is to get rid of your Ace and save your trump cards for the remaining hands to be played.

Hanging onto an Ace just because it is an Ace is no way to go through life.

BYZANTINE GENERALS | PLAY SOME EUCHRE

When Your Cards Turn to Crap Mid-Hand

Here's another example of when you might as well dump that Ace.

You had three hearts, including an Ace. But then the person who made trump, trumped your heart play. One thing you can know for certain, your other hearts are crap. Even if one of them is the Ace. You might as well use those cards for cannon fodder and save your remaining cards for later in the hand where they "might" be useful. Yes, even that ten.

Why?

Maybe the person that made trump will run out of them and play their nine on the final hand. If the other players have thrown their cards of that suit, you might have a chance to be the hero and get the stopper with that final, low card. Yes, it's a small chance. But your chance of playing that Ace and taking a trick has reached zero – so don't hang onto that Ace because it's an Ace.

When Do You Trump Your Partner's Ace?

Never.

BYZANTINE GENERALS | PLAY SOME EUCHRE

Exception: When you absolutely know that Ace isn't going around. For example, hearts have been played. Your partner took the trick *without* using the Ace – and then leads hearts back. If you know that your opponents have trump to play – see if they do. If they do, then obviously, over trump. If they don't – that's a judgement call: Do you think the person to your left will trump it? Do you want them to spend that trump card or do you want to spend a trump card to ensure capturing the trick.

This could be a lose-lose situation. You *don't* play trump and your opponent plays trump keeping you from sweeping all five tricks, or worse, getting euchred. Or you *do* play trump and your partner thinks you're an idiot because the person to your left threw junk on that Ace, which means you wasted a trump card.

Choose wisely.

Also: Never.

When Four Trump Isn't A Loner

Normally, you would look at this embarrassment of riches and think, "I should totally go alone." It "seems" obvious, considering you have the left bower and three other trump cards, right?

J♠ Q♣ 10♣ 9♣ J♦

Oh, but this one is deceiving. Realizing that the right bower beats your left bower, and the Ace and King of trump beats your Queen and Ten of trump. If those three cards are in a single hand, or even spread across your opponent's hands, going alone on this one there is the real possibility that you could get euchred. Then again, if any of those trap cards are buried in the kitty or buried in your partner's hand (if you go alone) maybe it will be ok. But then again, maybe you might be playing euchre outside of a laundromat in Waterton, Canada – eating a baloney sandwich, and make a call that goes down in euchre infamy as one of the worst calls ever made.

Other Scenarios

Now that you're caught up on what some of the basic strategies are, let's look at some scenarios and see how you do.

BYZANTINE GENERALS | PLAY SOME EUCHRE

Crap Hand with Lead

Your hand is crap. But you have the lead (Dealer is to your right). Your partner called hearts trump. Your only trump is the 9. What do you lead?

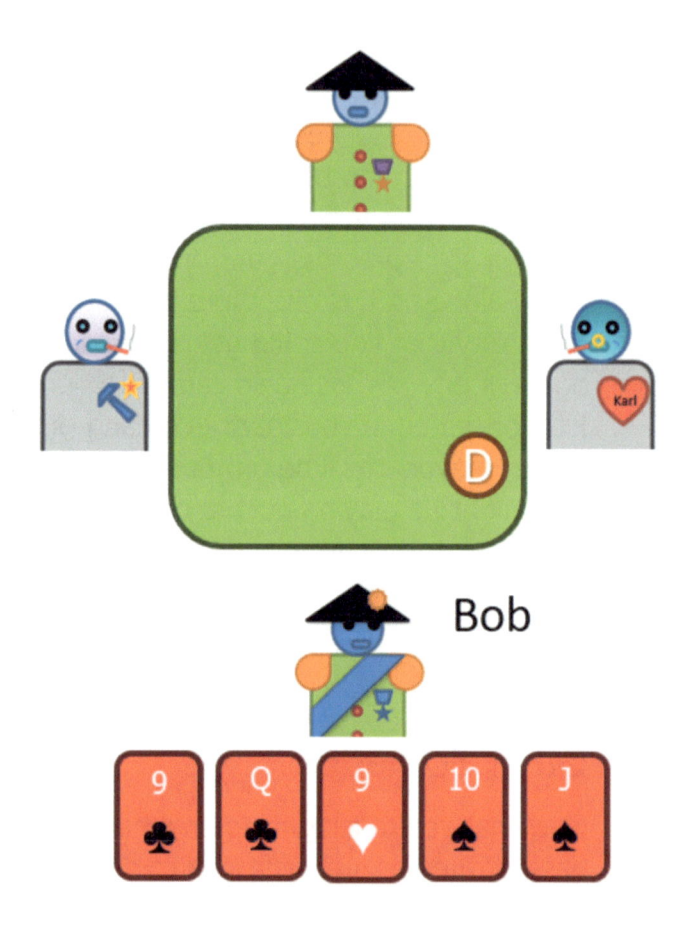

BYZANTINE GENERALS | PLAY SOME EUCHRE

Answer: The 9 of trump.

Your partner made trump, find out why. You're probably more of a spectator this hand, but your most important job right now is to give your partner an opportunity to take control.

Stuck – do you go left or right?

You have the following cards:

[9♣] [10♣] [J♠] [A♠] [A♦]

Do you call it spades or clubs?

Answer: Clubs.

Using the hand strength system that I outlined earlier - if you call spades, that's 2.5 points (two trump and the off-suit Ace). If you call clubs on the other hand, that's 4 points. Three trump and then both Aces become off-suit Aces.

Do you throw away that Ace?

In the example below, spades are trump. Your partner, Sam, is in control of the trick. Do you throw away the A♦ or use one of your trump cards?

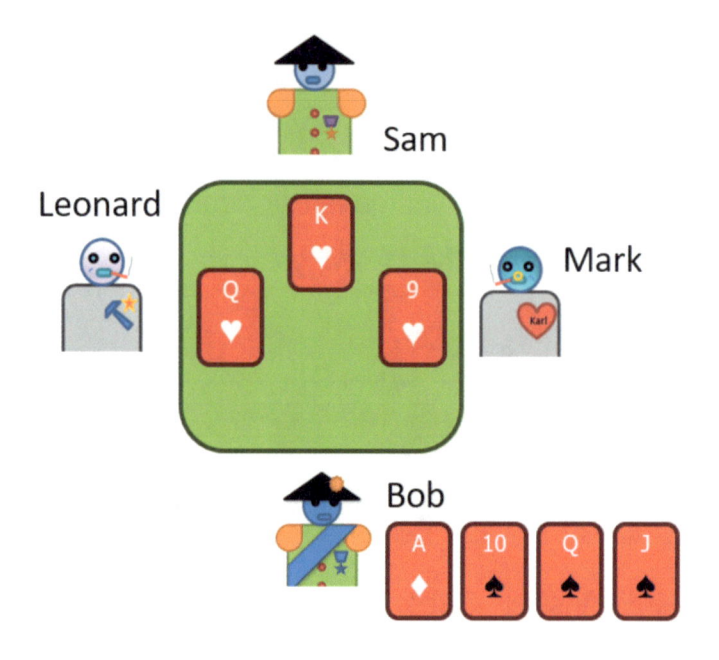

Answer: You throw away that Ace and save your trump cards.

Holding Four of the Same Suit with Lead

In this scenario your partner called trump. You had one trump card which you were able to use to take the trick. But now you don't have any more trump and you're holding four cards of the same suit, one of which is an Ace (shown in the

BYZANTINE GENERALS | PLAY SOME EUCHRE

figure below). Which one of your cards do you lead?

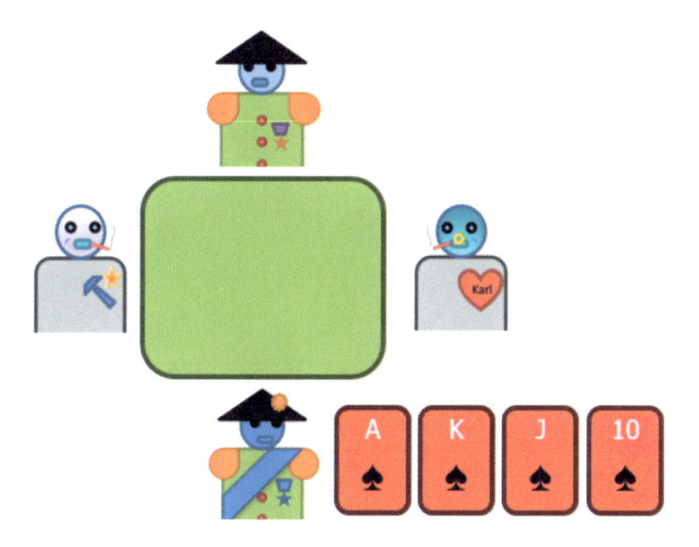

Answer: The 10♠. Why not Ace? Because the only other available spades are the Queen and the Nine. It is likely that if you lead the Ace, it will most likely get trumped. You don't want your partner thinking, "I shouldn't trump that Ace" because she thinks it won't get trumped. Play your low card signaling to your partner to take control of the hand. They called trump – you did your job by taking a trick – let them control the rest of the hand without any guesswork.

BYZANTINE GENERALS | PLAY SOME EUCHRE

Called Trump with No Bowers – What do you lead?

In this hand, you don't have any bowers, but you have three trump cards plus an off-suit Ace (as shown in the figure below). What do you lead?

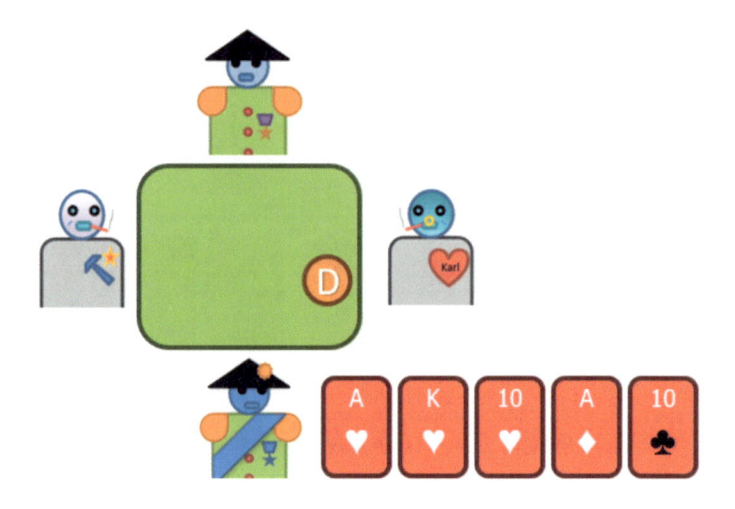

Answer: 10♥. You might lead the A♦ and get away with it as it is early in the hand, and everyone might have a diamond. Let's follow the guiding principle of "we made trump so lead trump." But the goal here is to find out where those bowers are. There are four other trump cards waiting in ambush – let's find them. Plus, if we pull the trump cards out early it makes it more likely that our off-suit Ace can be successfully played later without getting trumped. Playing the 10♥ is a low-cost way to go fishing for trump, saving our higher trump and that off-suit Ace for later in the hand.

Last Two Tricks – What to Lead?

In this scenario, your partner called Hearts trump. Your team has taken three tricks, so your point is guaranteed. You have the lead. You have the Q♥ and the Q♠.

What do you lead?

Answer: Q♠. You *could* lead the Q♥. That isn't horrible. It just isn't optimal given this scenario. Recall, your partner called trump. This may be an opportunity to get all five tricks. If you lead your trump queen, however, they will have to play what is likely their last trump card (if they had five trump cards it's not likely that you would have gotten the lead). In this scenario, your better play is the Q♠. This will give your partner an opportunity to trump that trick, saving your trump card for the final trick.

BYZANTINE GENERALS | PLAY SOME EUCHRE

Ordering your opponent's loner

This is the Grandpa Jake scenario that was alluded to in the dedication of this book. This one is simple – it just takes some guts to call it. Are you feeling lucky, punk? Well, are ya?

Sorry about going all Dirty Harry[1] on you for a second.

The dealer has a bower up. Whatever suit that is, you have a hand full of cards of the opposite color. For example, the Jack of Spades is up, and you have all Hearts in your hand. Or the Jack of Diamonds is up, and you have all Clubs in your hand.

In our previous discussions, almost everything has been based on the notion that from a situational awareness and risk basis, the cards are evenly distributed. However, in this scenario you're betting that the cards are *not* evenly distributed, based on the evidence in your hand. Certainly, for you – the cards are not evenly distributed.

What do you do? If you just sit there your opponent might go alone, shooting for 4 points.

---

[1] https://www.imdb.com/title/tt0066999/

BYZANTINE GENERALS | PLAY SOME EUCHRE

They might not. Maybe they are only going to go for 2.

Could this be a time that a "tell" matters? Did the dealer's eyes twitch when they looked into their hand and into the future? Did they declare that the State is all powerful?

This is the bet – that if *you* order it, they can *only* get the 2 points. The downside is that your opponent is going to get 2 points – you're just trying to keep them from getting the 4. Although maybe a miracle will happen, and your partner has all opposite cards from you in their hand, and *they* were going to call it.

Right – that was never going to happen.

If you're correct, and you order the trump (stopping the loner before it starts) both the person that was going to order it and your partner are going to be either (or both) pissed and amazed.

"Why did you order that?" Your partner will ask, accusingly.

"Why did you order that? I was going to go alone." Your opponent will ask with incredulity.

BYZANTINE GENERALS | PLAY SOME EUCHRE

The answer, dear reader, is simply because you are amazing and have reached the pinnacle of euchre expertise.

Final Thoughts

Just remember, you're never as good as you think you are. You could just be getting good cards. But you're also never as bad as your friends, family, coworkers, and acquaintances think you

BYZANTINE GENERALS | PLAY SOME EUCHRE

are... well, we should probably let time make the determination there.

Some people think that winning in euchre is just "luck." In my experience, what looks like luck in euchre is just the difference in a few points between how people play. Those decisions that are made in the moment, a single mistake against quality euchre players, can cost you. Those decisions are the difference between luck and skill.

Against people that think luck is a thing - they will never understand why it is that you seem to win more than you lose, how you are always able to stop a loner, stop a two-point hand, or squeak out a one-point hand when they think they have you. They will be mystified as to how you are able to turn a nothing hand into something, or what looks like a one-point hand (to them) into a loner hand.

BYZANTINE GENERALS | PLAY SOME EUCHRE

If you do make it to the highest echelons of skill, well, it turns out that maybe there is *some* luck involved. For example, our family tournament is set up as a round-robin wherein we play with each partner twice, and every set of partners plays every other set, which results in 16 rounds of euchre.

Every person is an expert euchre player. If you make a handful of mistakes; or, if too many of those 50/50 calls don't go your way, well, maybe the euchre gods weren't smiling on you. But it is also true that the higher your skill, the "luckier" you get.

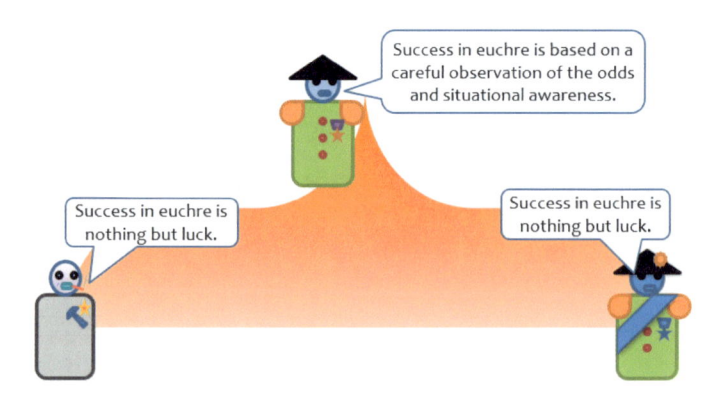

It turns out that luck is a journey. May you enjoy yours.

The Byzantine Generals Play Some Euchre

ISBN: 979-8-9882666-2-4

Made in the USA
Columbia, SC
02 June 2024